Deep Bay Relic

A Christian Mystery Suspense

By Kathleen Morris

This book is dedicated to all those enslaved in darkness. May you run from its shadows, turn from the relic, and follow the bright morning star into the brilliant light of day.

Book two in the Deep Bay Series

TABLE OF CONTENTS

Prologue

In the beginning...a flaming meteorite sliced through the heavens, leaving a smoky passageway to the waters below, inseminating the surface of the deep, infecting life with a foul ancient creature.

For years, it's been hiding in the 700-foot water-filled crater, waiting, lurking, and feeding on anything just to stay alive, never staying topside for long.

Until now.

Through the creatures small slits that served as its eyes, it saw the blurry mass floating above, waiting, hoping to catch a glimpse.

But the creature was not afraid, it roused at the movement in the shadows above, hopeful for a meal or two, ready to torpedo when least expected.

With the thrust of the creature's body, it quickly headed toward the surface, gaining speed as it neared the top. Then, as it broke through the water, freeing itself from the bondage it once knew, it birthed its ugly head.

The mass was no longer blurry but brilliant with color...and the creature was pleased with its efforts, thrilled to do it again and again until there was nothing left but a pool of crimson blood.

Chapter 1

Carla Reece took her scuba gear and headed for the boat with Mike, hoping that today wouldn't be as long as yesterday. They had been out all day and all evening and hadn't found anything that resembled treasure.

Being invited to go on a treasure hunt by her boyfriend was one thing, but Mike and his buddies seemed to be more interested in the Loch Ness Monster theories they kept talking about.

The word was, there were supposed to be monsters living in Deep Bay, or at least that's what the guys kept telling her, but she didn't believe that kind of thing. Why should she? She was older and wiser than all of them and knew a tale when she heard one.

Not even a child would believe it. When her kids were young, they always laughed whenever she told them about Santa Claus or the Tooth Fairy. Whenever Christmas came around, they teased her claiming *she* was both the Tooth Fairy and Santa.

What killjoys.

Carla had no one to blame but herself. She had taught her children to be sceptical, and now they didn't even believe in God.

Sometimes *she* even had trouble with that one. There were times when she would sit in church and just laugh under her breath at the Pastor. His sermons were so judgemental. In fact, most of the churches she had been to were full of judgemental hypocrites. That's why she stopped going to church altogether even though she had been a Christian ever since childhood.

Leaving church wasn't a decision she came upon lightly though, she'd prayed about it for a long time until the Lord revealed to her that she would be better off listening to Sunday services on television instead.

Now, at the age of 49, Carla never missed a televised Sunday morning service, and she still considered herself to be a Christian even though her good-for-nothing husband John, called her a heathen every time he left for church and she stayed at home.

He was the heathen with his judgmental attitude and his self-righteous phoney baloney persona he put on. Christians were supposed to love each other.

Their marriage had been falling apart for years, but more now since Casey, the youngest had moved out to go to College last year. They were practically divorced but still lived in the same house.

Actually, it all really started when she had an affair twenty years ago. She got pregnant with Casey. It wasn't something she was proud of, but what could she do? John was being a jerk as usual, and she was starving for love…just like now.

"Hey! Wake up Carla!" a voice rang out. "Are you daydreaming or something?"

Carla hadn't realized she was off in another world. They had already arrived at the diving point.

"Are you coming down or not?" Mike asked Carla rather rudely.

"I am!"

"Then move your butt, *Grandma!*"

"*Oh thanks!*" she laughed it off, wanting to say more but refraining because, after all, she *was* old enough to be a grandma. What was a 49-year-old woman doing with a 25-year-old guy anyway? She couldn't expect him to be respectful like older men, he was just a kid. The only thing she had going for her in this relationship was the *great* fringe benefits and the fact that he *wasn't* John.

Actually, she should count herself lucky, most women her age couldn't even find a man, leave alone one that still had hair on his head. But she *made* herself attractive, not like the average dowdy 49-year-old. She died her hair sandy blonde to cover the grey and spent a fortune on highlights every month. She always made sure she wore the latest styles as well, and the tanning salons gave her skin a healthy bronze glow. The liposuction and breast implants were a huge success, and the money spent on her face-lift last May was well worth it.

Carla made sure she was beautiful, in fact, she looked and felt twenty years younger. What man could pass her by without winking. Actually, that wasn't really the problem. She'd cheated on John for more than twenty years with anyone that wanted her, always telling herself that it was okay. The Bible said that husbands should love their wives like Christ loved the Church – John failed at that so many times – so it wasn't *her* fault she strayed from him. How was she supposed to get the love she needed?
John's churchy friends had a lot of names for her. None of them nice. That was okay with her though, God knew her struggles and she was *sure* he accepted her anyway.

As Carla slipped her wet suit over her tiny pink bikini and zipped it over her large implants, she sighed at the realization that Mike had already dove down with his four buddies. Why did she feel like the fifth wheel here? Hadn't they had enough treasure hunting for one week?

She spit into her mask like Mike had showed her, rubbing it around the glass so it wouldn't fog up, and slipped it over her tanned face, climbing down the ladder on the side of the boat, submerging her black flippers into the cold dark water.

As she lowered her entire body, put her breathing apparatus over her mouth and took one last look around her before going all the way underwater, something startled her. She ripped her gear off her face immediately and climbed back up the ladder, breathing hard. *There's something in the water!*

Carla didn't know if she was seeing things or if the water actually had turned a different color. She looked again, squinting in the sun, cupping a hand over her brow so that she could see a little better.

She *was* right, her mind confirmed. The water *is* red!

~~~

It was mid morning and Sadie Long was frying eggs for the two guests that still hadn't gotten up yet. The five divers with the boat had taken off early again with nothing for breakfast but a case of beer. It bothered her that they even brought it along with them since they were told that this was a dry resort. She'd have to call in for reinforcements to deal with the issue. It happened every now and then.

Shining Star Lodge was a Christian establishment, it had been since it opened for business four years ago. Everybody knew it, or at least she thought they did. It even said so on their brochure.

Sadie inhaled the aroma from the crackling eggs in the frying pan. Oh, how she loved the smell of fried eggs in the morning. It reminded her of her days as a school teacher. She'd make breakfast every morning for the children who came to school hungry. It was her own little outreach program that meant so much to her at the time.

She still missed that part of her life, but she was glad she wasn't teaching anymore. It was getting so difficult to do her job properly in an ungodly school system these days. The kids were becoming so unruly and it was hard to enforce discipline on them especially when their parents thought they were angels.

Teaching in a Christian school appealed to her but Sadie couldn't seem to acquire a permanent position. All she could manage to get were substitute positions, and she couldn't pay the bills doing that.

Never marrying didn't help matters either. Perhaps if she had a husband, she wouldn't have had to struggle with money all her life. At least that's what her friends always told her. But Sadie never had the desire to get married. Sure, she liked men, but she invested her time into her teaching career when she was young, and then all the *good* ones were snatched away before she even had a chance. The ones she did date, always seemed to want one thing, and she wouldn't give them *that*. She would not compromise her faith for a roll in the hay. It just wasn't worth it.

In return for her obedience, Sadie always felt blessed. She was content just being single, doing God's work – and when the opportunity arose for her to take on The Shining Star Ministries it was an honour.

Leading Bible Study classes at a wilderness retreat fit her like a glove. God knew all along what He wanted Sadie Long to do with her life. She may not have a husband, but those who came to Shining

Star always provided her with enough love and companionship to last a lifetime.

Except the five divers, that is.

Sadie wondered why they were here. They weren't like the usual guests who would come to the resort. They seemed to be after something. And the older woman who tagged along with them didn't quite fit, with her Barbie looking physique and her long pink gel nails. It was clear she was trying to fool everyone into thinking she wasn't aging, but Sadie saw it in her eyes. She was old and worn, probably almost as old as she was. No makeup and hairdo could cover up *that*. She wondered why some women fought aging so much. Sadie just accepted her plain Jane looks. God made her just the way He wanted, and that's the way she would stay.

Perhaps the woman needed to hear the same thing, but Sadie hadn't had the opportunity to say much of anything to her since her arrival a week ago. She would always run out early with those boys and return late at night. But that didn't matter, they were supposed to be staying another week. If God wanted her to reach out to this woman, He would give her the opportunity. He always did.

Sadie put the last minute touches on the two breakfast platters that were now ready to eat. All she had to do was ring the bell and her two guests would come running like they always did.

Eunice had been at Shining Star now for the last two months. Life was hard for her. She had been sponsored by her church to come and stay as long as she needed, but Sadie wondered if she was making any progress at all.

It wasn't her place to judge, just teach God's word, but she'd hoped for more progress by now.

Each evening they had a Bible Study together and it was only last week that Eunice finally shared with the group about her problems.

One of her problems was beginning to show long before the woman ever spoke a word. Even though Sadie had never had children of her own, she knew when someone was pregnant. Eunice couldn't hide it any longer, in fact, that was the straw that broke the camel's back so to speak. She must have realized people weren't blind.

At first, Sadie just listened. Eunice had quite a story. She actually *was* a believer, a very strong believer, but like so many women, she got caught up with the wrong man. Now, after ten years of common-law marriage to a catholic man, and four kids later, she was stuck in a sinful situation.

"But I *can't* leave him!" she would cry over and over. "I tried *many* times. My church even tried to help me get out of the relationship, but I couldn't leave my children. Sin is sin, I know that, but what about the innocent children? They didn't ask to be part of this. Should I punish them for *my* sins?"

Sadie never knew how to answer her. All she could ever think of was Eve, and her sin of taking the apple. Hadn't her children had to pay for *her* sins? Even now, all the sons and daughters of Eve were still paying for her sins.

But Sadie couldn't tell her that. For some reason, her mouth wouldn't open whenever she tried to explain it. She prayed for wisdom everyday for this situation with Eunice. It was definitely a tough one.

And now she was pregnant with a fifth child. Sadie's heart broke for her especially when she told her of her journey to the abortion clinic one day. It must have been tough on the woman but she was glad she decided to keep the child. Life is precious to God. That advice she did give her, but advice about her family situation was not so easy.

Sadie wondered just how far along Eunice was in her pregnancy, she told her six months or so, but over the past three weeks, it looked more like nine. Maybe that's because of her cooking.

That reminded her of the eggs, they were getting cold.

"Eunice says she isn't hungry, Sadie," a voice shot out from around the corner. It was Dinah, a teenage girl sent to Shining Star from another church. She was only seventeen and had already been through the ringer.

At the tender age of thirteen, she was raped by her mother's boyfriend. Her home environment wasn't exactly stable. After that, she fell into prostitution and got hooked on crystal meth. If it hadn't been for the local church and their street ministry, she wouldn't have had a chance. They sent her to a drug rehabilitation facility, and then they sent her to Shining Star Lodge.

Sadie led her to the Lord the first week she arrived, and now after setting her up with a Christian group home called, Broken Wing, she was almost ready to go.

A tear came to her eye. How could she let her little butterfly go? That's what she called the pixie-faced blonde with freckles each time she hugged her…just like now.

"You're squeezing me too tight again," Dinah groaned, locked in Sadie's bear-hug, smiling through her tears as she kissed the girl on the top of her head.

"My butterfly."

"Okay already, *I'm your butterfly*," Dinah groaned again, "but didn't you hear me? I said

Eunice isn't coming for breakfast, she says she isn't hungry, but I know she has to be, you saw how many snacks she had last night before bed."

"Maybe that's *why* she isn't hungry, dear."

"I don't think so. I heard her bawling last night. I couldn't sleep a wink."

"I know sweetheart," Sadie frowned, "I heard her too. We just have to keep praying for her. God will help her in his own gentle way. Just like you. Now bow your head with me so we can eat these eggs before they get too cold."

As Dinah prayed for the meal, Sadie opened one eye and peered through the large kitchen window toward the Star River in front of the lodge. A boat was coming in.

"Eat up dear," Sadie said, excusing herself from the table. "I'll be right back. I just have to go see who that is coming in with the boat."

"It's probably those strange diver people."

Sadie just shook her head, hearing the girl but not turning to respond, focussing more on the strangeness of the situation.

"Oh, and by the way," Dinah shouted with a mouthful of eggs. "Those four guys have been flirting with me like crazy."

Sadie stopped then, turned to Dinah with a great big frown.

Giggling, the girl blurted out with laughter, "Just kidding. You looked so serious I had to do something."

"You just finish eating young lady," Sadie scolded her. "Just don't joke about that kind of thing. It's not funny."

Dinah was still grinning when she turned to finish her meal. The girl was such a tease. But right now, Sadie wasn't in the mood. Something was wrong, she could feel it.

As the boat neared the small dock, Sadie rushed over to it, wiping her sweaty hands in her full apron that was still tied around her from cooking breakfast.

"Hello," she shouted, waving her arms to the lone occupant. As she got closer, she realized it was the diving woman. But where were the others?

The woman jumped out of the boat and tied it up to the dock. She flopped like a rag doll down to the grass beside the dock and moaned, "Help me! Please!"

"What is it?" Sadie rushed up to the woman, bending down beside her.

The woman looked a mess. Her black wet-suit was shiny and wet, and her bare feet were all bloody. The black smudged eyeliner under her eyes made her tanned face look like a zombie.

"What happened?" Sadie asked, lowering her voice to a soothing tone, stroking the woman's bushy hair. The woman relaxed a bit but was obviously still upset.

"They're dead," she sobbed against Sadie's shoulder. "They're *all* dead!"

Chapter 2

It was just before lunch when Brian received the call.

Just the thought of going back there, gave him a stomach ache. It had been a long time, four years to be exact. He hoped he'd never have to go up there again, but he needed the money, and his private investigation business wasn't doing very well since they moved to Prince Albert.

He had decided the police force wasn't what he wanted for his family any more. Shortly after the Shooting Star Lodge incident five years ago, he called it quits. The murders and crime spree that went on at Deep Bay, not to mention almost losing his own life, made him realize he wasn't spending enough time with the people he loved.

Freelancing was the option he took, but not until he and his boss got together to decide what to do with the Shooting Star Lodge – a gift from his boss's best friend who happened to own the lodge. His friend was brutally murdered during the same crime spree that almost ended Brian's life. He willed the deed to his boss who in turn sold it to him.

"I don't know what to do with the property yet," Brian told his boss, "but I know someone who might."

It was at that time that Brian and his wife took off to Vancouver for Harvey and Loretta's wedding. They almost lost their lives in the Shooting Star incident as well. Loretta's son had been murdered in a bank robbery and the killers fled to Deep Bay. Her testimony in the case helped close many other cold cases across the U.S and Canada. He was thankful for that, but very sure he never wanted to step foot in Shooting Star Lodge ever again, and neither did Harvey and Loretta.

But that soon changed.

After spending time in Vancouver with Harvey, Brian started realizing his friend had something, some shiny quality about him that made him comfortable to be around. And it wasn't just because he was getting married, it was something else.

Then as Harvey simply told him the reason why, Brian wanted to know more about it. Loretta and his wife Jenny had been out shopping that day it happened. It was a fond memory – a changing moment in his life.

Harvey helped Brian pray a prayer of forgiveness, and invite Jesus to live in his heart. His new friend helped him realize he was a sinner and brought him to his knees. For that, he is forever grateful.

When Loretta and Jenny returned from their shopping trip, they were bubbling with excitement. At first, he wondered how they could have known what he and Harvey were talking about, and then he realized Jenny had found the Lord too.

It was a completely different way of living for them both, but exciting at the same time. He and Jenny wanted to change their lives, start going to church, and reading the Bible. It was just something that felt natural to them.

Then it all came together the day of Harvey and Loretta's wedding. Harvey came rushing over to him with his black tux on, a half hour before the wedding was about to start. He went and got Loretta, already dressed in her white wedding gown, and then the four of them had a meeting. As odd as it was, it was all planned out by God.

"I know what to do with the lodge," Harvey blurted with excitement, kissing his bride to be.

"Control yourself Harvey," Loretta smiled.

"I can't," he continued. "The Lord told me what to do. He *told* me what to do."

"Okay," Loretta smirked, "then spit it out."

"Well," he went on, "So many lives were lost at Shooting Star Lodge, right? So many bad things happened to all of us out there. The devil had a real heyday. So, let's put a stop to that. Let's turn it around and use it for God. Our church is looking for ways to invest in some kind of ministry and this could be just the way. We could burn that awful shack to the ground and build a brand new one right on the same spot, except this time, it will be for God. Churches could sponsor people with problems, young people, old people, anyone that needs help. They could send them there to get spiritual training. It doesn't have to be big. Something small and personable – and I know the perfect person to run it. Loretta and I met her in our Bible Study group. She's been praying for God to direct her life. She's *already* a teacher. Her name is Sadie Long. Wonderful gal. And I even have a name for the new place: *Shining* Star Lodge."

For a moment, everyone was stunned.

It was amazing that Harvey had enough breath to say all that in one mouthful, but that's not why what he said had left everyone speechless, it was because it was such a perfect idea.

"You're amazing sweetheart," Loretta smiled and kissed Harvey. Tears ran down her cheeks. "*This* is why I love this man."

"I hope you know this means we will all have to go back there then," Brian frowned, breaking the mood.

Harvey held up his hands. "One thing at a time my friend. First, Loretta and I have a wedding to get to, and then we're going on a long honeymoon. Then, we'll deal with the new venture. We'll call you when we have everything set up with the church. Then we'll take a trip to Deep Bay again – a very short trip."

And he kept his word as Brian knew his old friend would. The memory was bittersweet, still etched in the corner of his mind.

"Come on honey!" his wife interrupted his thoughts. "If you don't hurry, you're going to miss your plane."

Brian shook his head. "All these memories Jen, it's hard to forget."

"Are you okay? Maybe I *should* go with you."

"I told you that wasn't necessary, and besides, you have to stay home with the boys."

"Patrick is 18-year-old, he can watch his little brother?"

He didn't want his wife to come along, but how could he get that through her head. The last place he wanted to take her was Deep Bay. She had come out with him briefly when they burned the lodge down and hired the crew to build the new one. He hoped that would be the last time he had to take her up there.

Jenny stood there in front of him with her arms crossed in front of her chest waiting for him to respond to her question that by now Brian knew was actually a statement. "Of course, Patrick can baby-sit Nathan, but can't you just stay home? I need you to stay home."

Jenny looked sideways at him. "Alright, but...I'll be praying for you every minute, and if you change your mind, just give me a call. You know I'll hop on the first plane if you need me."

"I know."

He gave his wife a kiss and a long hug and grabbed his suitcase and his wallet and headed for the door. "Oh," he said, "one more thing. If anyone calls me for a case, just take their number. I'll get back to them as soon as I can. I don't know how long this case will take me. The woman was very vague. All she said was she needed me to find her boyfriend who went missing this morning. Sadie vouched for her – so that's basically the only reason I took the case, that, and the fact that the woman said that money was no object. She just wanted to find her boyfriend. It'll be good to see Sadie again too. It's been about four years now, hasn't it honey?"

"Yes Brian," Jenny grinned pushing him out the door. "Now quit jabbering and get going. You really *are* going to miss that plane if you don't hurry."

~~~~

The group of men laughed so hard they could hardly catch their breath.

"I'm sorry kid," Mike roared. "We didn't mean to leave you out of the loop, but I had to get the old lady off my back for at least one day. She was getting on my nerves."

"You didn't have to leave a trail of blood with that fish you cut up," the kid complained. "The creature won't like it."

The three fools didn't know anything, they only thought of money and their harebrained scheme to catch the monster on film. Little did they know that it wasn't as easy as they thought. It hid far beyond the underwater caves they were now relaxing in.

"Do you think she thinks I'm dead?" Mike giggled, spitting out his beer through his mouth and nostrils as he lay stretched out on a slimy rock with his wetsuit still on.

"She's a bimbo," Adam, the dark haired one remarked. "What else would she think? Even a drop of blood would make her faint, and you left a whole pool of it right by the ladder, you old dog you."

More laughter resounded through the underwater caves, giving them just enough air to carry on the way they were, obviously drunk on the beer they brought with them.

It was sickening.

The larger one in the back nicknamed Cutter was rolling around on the slime green rock with his black wetsuit, he looked like a big black seal for a minute. If he wasn't careful, his drunken stupor would land him right back in the water.

They made course derogatory jokes about Carla, making fun of the way she looked, laughing at her too tanned face and long witch nails. It was horrible to listen to a man that obviously was just using the woman for one thing.

"What's your problem kid?" Mike blurted out as he sat up, noticing he wasn't laughing along with them. "Don't you people have a sense of humour?"

You people?

"I have a sense of humour," the kid whispered back.

Just not like you.

Mike grinned and continued questioning the young man. "You know kid, when you work with us you have to stay with us, laugh with us, drink with us, and cuss with us. We told you that when we hired you. Didn't we tell you that?"

No answer.

"Maybe we should just fire him," Cutter snickered.

"No," Mike put up a hand to quiet Cutter. "We hired him because he said he was a guide, a *native* guide who knew Deep Bay better than any white man, and we're going to hold him to his word. Didn't you tell us that kid?

"Yes."

"Then you better show us where this Loch Ness Monster is before we start doing something drastic. It's been a week already and we just found this cave today. Maybe we're just wasting our time and money on you."

"No," the kid blurted out quickly. "I know these waters but you have to be patient. The monster is unpredictable – It sometimes takes a while to find him."

"Fine," Mike said, "we'll wait, but you better not be stringing us along or we'll have to *kill* you."

The kid's eyes grew wide.

"Just kidding kid," Mike grinned, teasing him some more. "You know that, don't you buddy? You're not a baby, are you?"

"I'm eighteen."

"Oh," Cutter teased, "the kid *is* a baby."

Mike reached into his backpack for something and fished around. "Here it is," he said. "I knew we had one more for you kid. By the way, what's your name anyway? We've been calling you kid for a week and I'm sick of it. Don't you have a name?"

"Pip."

They all burst out with roaring laughter. "What was that?" Cutter teased again. "Did he say his name was *Pippi Longstocking?*"

"It's *Pip*," he said getting mad now. "It's short for Pipata."

"Hold on Cutter," Mike stopped his friends bantering and took on a more serious tone. "If he says his name is *not* Pippi Longstocking, then it's not Pippi Longstocking. He was man enough to tell us his name as girlish as it is, so in return I think that we can share our beer with him. Here you go *Pip*."

Mike tossed the beer over to Pip and he caught it but he wasn't about to drink it. His old friend Grayling once told him, "Drink with a wise man, and you will become very wise, but drink with a fool and you will be one also." Those words stuck with Pip since his childhood, and he carried them with him ever since.

With the jagged rock-edge Pip popped off the bottle-cap and pretended to take a swig of beer. He forced a grin when the others cheered, doing the same thing again and again, pouring it out into the water a little at a time when they weren't looking. It was so dark in there except for the flashlights they had on, that they could hardly see what he was doing anyway.

It didn't take long for them to pass out. Before he knew it, Pip could hear them snoring, especially Cutter with his big belly rising and falling as he slept.

Suddenly, Pip heard something echo through the distant caves. He knew what that familiar hissing sound was, and he was going after it, but not with them.

Alone.

Chapter 3

"How long did you say you've been running this place?" Carla asked as she sat on the couch with the other two women, checking the bandages on her big toe. She wished she hadn't stubbed it on the edge of the boat. She bled like a stuck pig.

"Four years," the woman answered back as she walked into the room carrying a black book in her arms. "The best four years of my life."

"And you run it all by yourself?" Carla continued to Drill her.

"Just me and the Lord."

Carla was beginning to get the vibe that something was a little strange. From her experience, people that felt they needed to talk about the Lord constantly, were either so insecure with themselves, or fruitcakes. This woman was beginning to make her think the latter was the case here.

"And you don't get lonely?" Carla had to ask. If it were her running this place, she wouldn't last a week.

"Nope," the woman smiled through her coffee stained teeth and her ratty grey hair she probably hadn't combed since last week. She could do with a little makeup and some deodorant, but for some reason, Carla knew it wouldn't matter much. The woman was obviously some kind of bush woman. Her unshaven legs and burly crop of dark underarm hair that poked out of her sleeveless nightgown made that point clear as a bell.

Carla tried not to stare so she darted her eyes away quickly and took out her file to manicure her pink nails, snuggling up with the crocheted blanket next to her. The roaring fire in the fireplace made the room feel cozy and warm.

"Would you look at that?" she blurted out, peering at her hand, trying to break the silence in the room. "I broke a nail. I can't believe it. I spent fifty bucks on these things."

The young teenage girl on the other side of the couch leaned over to take a closer look, and then shrugged without saying a word.

Suddenly, the room grew quieter than it was before and Carla watched the bush woman open a book in her lap. "We usually have a Bible study before bed," the woman told her."

Wonderful. Perhaps this would give her an idea as to how fanatical these people were. Thankfully, she had come home late with Mike every day this week, and she hadn't had to endure the woman's preaching until now.

The woman introduced herself as Sadie, and the other two were Eunice and Dinah. "I'm Carla," she told them, thinking afterward that she probably shouldn't have said her name with such enthusiasm. Now they would think she was actually going to participate in this study.

Little did she know that Sadie had intended to quiz her.

"So, what brings you to our lodge Carla?"

At first, she didn't realize the woman was speaking to her, then she saw that they were all waiting with bug eyes for her to answer the question. "My boyfriend invited me. He likes to go diving in the bay. He's nuts about it actually. I hope he's alright. Do you think he is?"

"I'm sure he's fine," Sadie soothed her. "My friend Brian is a good Private Investigator. He'll find your boyfriend for you as soon as his plane arrives in the morning."

"I hope so."

The gigantic pregnant lady in the recliner fidgeted in her chair. She was an odd one. Her eyes were so puffy and red she looked like she had been crying for a week. It took her off guard when she actually asked Carla a question.

"Are you married?" Eunice asked her bluntly.

Carla sat there stunned, then she looked at her wedding band still on her finger, and hid her hand. "What makes you think I'm married. I told you I came here with my boyfriend."

"I saw your wedding ring."

It was safe to say that Eunice was not going to be any friend of Carla's in the near future. She had already stuck her nose where it didn't belong. "So what," she grinned like a Cheshire cat. "A girl can have a little fling or two, can't she?"

Eunice glared at her and shook her head in silence.

Sadie began to rub her forehead, obviously uncomfortable with the conversation. "Let's change the subject shall we," she forced a grin. "First, I would like to welcome you to our Bible study group Carla and tell you that we are believers in Jesus Christ. Have you ever heard the Gospel before?"

My whole life. "Actually," Carla said clearing her throat ready to tell them a thing or two about what she knew. It was hard not to boast about how much she knew about the Bible but *she* asked for it. This was going to be a piece of cake.

"Actually, I *am* a Christian," Carla continued, smug as ever. "I accepted Jesus into my heart at the age of four and I've been a believer ever since. I can probably quote more scripture verses than all of you put together."

"Is that right?" Eunice snapped at her. "How about the seventh commandment miss high and mighty – '*Thou shalt not commit adultery*!' I bet you didn't even know that one was *in* the Bible."

"I beg your pardon," Carla fumed. If she wanted a fight, she was going to get one. "Who made you my judge?"

"Me!" Eunice shouted, crawling out of the recliner in a hurry.

"That's *enough* girls!" Sadie tried to stop it but it was too late.

"This *very* commandment has been shoved in my face for FIFTEEN LONG YEARS," Eunice said, crying now. "I've felt sick each and every time I chose to break this law. I've struggled more than *anybody* could *ever* imagine because of my sin and you come waltzing in here claiming that it's perfectly okay to have your cake and eat it too. You make me sick. You profess to be a Christian yet you appear to have no remorse for breaking the very laws that you're supposed to live by. If that's not a double standard, then I don't know what is."

Carla felt her face go red. Eunice stood there in front of her chair, hands on her hips ready for battle. "You don't even know me lady," she spit. "You can't judge me."

"I know you!" Eunice shook with anger. "I've known people like you my whole life. You're just like me. The only difference is *I'm* actually sorry for what I've done wrong. But you know what, it doesn't make a difference. I still have to live with the *scars*, and so do you no matter how much you try to cover it up."

The woman was getting on her nerves. "I'm not covering anything up," Carla snapped back. "And you have no right to accuse me, or judge my life. God knows my struggles and He accepts me just the way that I am."

"So, no remorse then," Eunice chuckled in anger. "You can basically do whatever you want as a Christian without any worries. I guess that answers all my questions then. According to you I have no problems at all."

"What?" This was all so confusing. Eunice made no sense whatsoever. Carla was glad she wasn't the one that was pregnant. The woman's hormones were obviously running her mouth into overtime.

Eunice glared at Carla, mute for a minute. Her heavy breathing pierced the silent room. "You know what?" Eunice flung her arms up in surrender. "I give up. I'm done with this whole stinkin' discussion. I'm going to bed."

Good riddance!

She shuffled passed the couch where Carla and Dinah still sat and said one last thing before she left the room. "You guys...you go *right* ahead and study whatever it is that you *hypocrites* want ...and you can do it without *me*. I've had enough of it."

With that said, she stomped to her room and slammed her bedroom door, leaving the air so thick, you could cut a knife straight through it.

Sadie whispered under her breath, apparently praying to herself. Carla gulped and looked around the room. Dinah hung her head in silence.

"What? It's not *my* fault she snapped," Carla finally blurted out what she thought the other two women must be thinking of her.

"No," Sadie answered with a sigh. "It's not your fault. Eunice has a lot of issues to deal with right now, and I'm afraid you were her punching bag tonight. I'm sorry for her outbursts. Our Bible studies aren't usually so...intense. Please don't let this incident ruin our chances to get to know each other while you're here. We would love to have you join our Bible study again tomorrow night if you're still around."

Definitely not. Spending time with those three women was the last thing Carla wanted to do. Women like Eunice, and their snotty attitudes, were the very reasons she chose to watch sermons on T.V instead of going to church. Judgmental people made her sick. Hopefully, the P.I would find Mike safe and sound in the morning and she could finally get out of this crazy place.

~~~~~

Sadie pulled the covers over her head and tried to drown out the awful bawling sounds coming through her bedroom wall again. Eunice would be keeping them up yet another night and all because of that silly argument.

She wished she would have been able to stop the two women. Their argument was full of disrespect and hypocrisy, and a poor way to start a Bible study. No wonder Carla and Dinah left the room after that.

If only she could go to Eunice right now and calm her down, maybe they'd all be able to sleep tonight. But Sadie knew it was hopeless, she tried it before but Eunice always told her to go away. You can't help someone who doesn't want to be helped.

Carla troubled her too. Why did she have to give Eunice the impression that sin was okay? It was heartbreaking. Sadie knew that there was no exception for sin. Why couldn't she say that when she needed to?

The night had been a complete failure.

What would Jesus have said to Carla had He been in the room tonight? Hopefully it would be the same thing Sadie *wished* she would have said, the same thing Jesus said to the adulterous woman caught by teachers of the law and Pharisees in John chapter 8.

Sadie flipped through her Bible and found the story, reading John 8:1-11: *"Jesus went to the Mount of Olives. At dawn he appeared again in the temple courts, where all the people gathered around him, and he sat down to teach them. The teachers of the law and the Pharisees brought in a woman caught in adultery. They made her stand before the group and said to Jesus. "Teacher, this woman was caught in the act of adultery. In the Law Moses commanded us to stone such women. Now what do you say? They were using this question as a trap, in order to have a basis for accusing him.*

But Jesus bent down and started to write on the ground with his finger. When they kept on questioning him, he straightened up and said to them, "If any one of you is without sin, let him be the first to throw a stone at her." Again, he stooped down and wrote on the ground.

At this, those who heard began to go away one at a time, the older ones first, until only Jesus was left, with the woman still standing there. Jesus straightened up and asked her, "Woman, where are they? Has no one condemned you?"

"No one, sir," she said.

"Then neither do I condemn you." Jesus declared. "Go now and leave your life of sin.""

Sadie grinned. *There* was her answer. "*Go now and leave your life of sin.*" This verse was what she was looking for. Why hadn't she been able to think of it when she needed it?

Most people use this story as a basis to show that we're all sinners so we shouldn't judge others. This is true, but it isn't the only message in the story. Sure, we aren't to judge, we're all filthy sinners, but...we *are* to leave our lives of sin.

A light bulb went on inside Sadie's head. Jesus didn't condemn the adulterous woman, but he didn't excuse her sin either. He didn't shrug his shoulders and say, "Oh well," like Carla did. He told her to leave her life of sin.

She wished she could turn back the clock and give the women a *real* Bible study on this. She would tell them, "Jesus wants to forgive *any* sin we do in our lives. He wants us to be repentant and change our hearts for Him."

Oh, how good it sounded now, after the fact. It would have taught them so much. All she needed to say was, "If we call ourselves believers, we have to act like it. We can't go around breaking God's laws as if we *don't* believe. We need to repent...and repentance means we want to change –leave our lives of sin."

Sadie was getting tired now, her yawning broke her train of thought. She'd been at it now for two hours and it was time to close the Bible up and go to sleep. Eunice had even stopped bawling.

Lord, please give me another chance to teach these women what your words say.

As the digital clock beside the bed clicked over to 2 a.m. Sadie bent to switch the light off. She finished her prayers and snuggled down to sleep, remembering that the morning would come early, and with it, a whole new set of problems.

Chapter 4

The early morning sun kissed down on Reindeer Lake as Brian watched the plane motor over to the landing dock on Star River. It was just around the corner from Deep Bay and a short walking distance to Shining Star Lodge.

Memories flooded back to him from the first time he set eyes on this place. It was the most beautiful scenery he had ever seen. Precambrian volcanic rock formations edged the vast shores of Reindeer Lake, one of the biggest bodies of water in Northern Saskatchewan.

Deep Bay was the most remarkable part of the lake. It was said to have formed from an enormous meteorite when the earth was still in its infantile stage, but legend had it that monsters lived in that part of the lake. Brian grinned to himself, sea creatures, the Loch Ness Monsters, and Big Foot stories always seemed to have a way of popping up around the world. It never ceased to amaze him at how many people actually believed in these types of fairy tails.

A sense of déjà vu came over him as he jumped out of the plane and waved goodbye to the pilot, watching him take off into the blush of morning. He had flown himself up here the first time, and vowed never to do that again. Each time he came up now, he always took a charter. Too many memories to trust himself to fly. Even now the sick feeling started coming back to him.

This is different.

Brian shook his head and concentrated on the beautiful scenery. The tall pines stood like matriarchs in front of him, welcoming him, calming his jittery nerves. If he hadn't experienced such trauma in this place, one would never think this pristine wilderness could hide so much evil like it did five years ago, the first time he was here.

This time is different.

He had to get his mind on something else while he walked the trail to the Shining Star Lodge or it would eat him up inside. *Lord, clear my mind.*

With his briefcase full of legal documents for his new client, he hurried along with it, knowing that the big nine-millimetre attached to his hip would come in handy if he had to use it. *This time is different.*

Just in case, he kept his hand close to the revolver. A Private Investigator should always be prepared. Being on the police force taught him that much, even though it was never needed most of the time.

Having a live case this time around excited Brian. Most of his cases were cold murder cases he usually found at the R.C.M.P detachment. He'd investigate the cold case and collect the bounty. Most of the time it paid pretty good. His last reward was $50,000 for solving the murder of Arnold Johnson, killed by a single gunshot wound to the left temple and found in a dumpster in Trenton, Ontario. It was a hard case to crack, and it cost him most of the bounty with the endless plane fare, motel rooms, and stakeouts half across the country, but he still made enough money to pay the bills.

Maybe a local case would actually boost his career in the area. Prince Albert was a small city and he didn't get many cases. The police handled most of what came up.

As Brian rounded the corner he had to stop in awe. The Shining Star Lodge stood there before him with such tranquil beauty, just the way he remembered it, thankful they had burnt the old one down to the ground.

With the rising sun in his eyes, Brian stood at the door about to knock.

"My old friend!" a warm jovial voice greeted him as the door opened before he even had a chance to knock. "Come in. It's good to see you again!"

The smell of Sadie's special home ground coffee wafted through the front door as Brian entered the lodge. He inhaled the inviting smell as he gave the thin woman a hug.

"This must be hard for you," Sadie said, pulling from the embrace, staring straight into his teary eyes.

This time is different. "I'm fine Sadie," he sniffled, feeling foolish. "You always do this to me."

"Men can cry you know," she teased, leading him into the kitchen for her famous cup of coffee.

But they weren't supposed to. "I know," he grinned sheepishly, trying to change the subject as quickly as he could.

"So, where's the client?"

"Way to change the subject Mr. Tough Guy."

Brian blushed in silence as he pulled his briefcase to the countertop and clicked it open. He took out the thin laptop, and a few papers, trying to look as professional as possible while Sadie poured him a dark cup of coffee.

His old friend pulled up a chair and grabbed her own cup to join him. "She's still sleeping. We can visit a while until she wakes up. It'll give me time to get caught up with you and Jen. What have you two been up to lately? How's Patrick and Nathan doing?"

All these questions came at once. Sadie was a wonderful woman and a pleasure to have as a sister in Christ, but he forgot what she was like. She'd talk you to death.

"Jen's still doing nursing. She enjoys it. Patrick's going to try Bible School in the fall, Nathan's growing, and I'm still holding the fort with my P.I business. How about you?"

Sadie went on about the many visitors she'd had at the lodge over the last few years, telling him that it's been a joy to do the Lords work. "Another cup?" she asked him in mid sentence."

"No," he said, looking at his watch. "I would actually like to get going on this investigation. I don't want the morning to slip by before I even get started."

"I'm *here*!" a voice shouted from down the hall.

A tall middle-aged woman that seemed to be overdressed for a wilderness lodge sauntered over to them and shook Brian's hand. "You must be the private investigator."

For a minute, Brian thought she actually winked. He cleared his throat and introduced himself. "I need to ask you several questions Carla, and have you sign some papers before we do anything else. I hope you don't mind."

Brian wanted to get right down to business with this woman. She seemed to be a little over-friendly with him and he didn't like it one bit.

Throughout the verbal investigation with Carla Reece, Brian began to realize he had arrived unprepared. "Why didn't you tell me on the phone that he went missing while scuba-diving in Deep Bay?"

"I don't know," the woman replied.

Brian turned toward Sadie.

"I'm sorry Brian," Sadie said, "I assumed she told you."

Carla fidgeted. "Is this a problem?"

Is this a problem? Of course, this was a problem. Brian didn't have the equipment or the manpower to follow through with a dive investigation. There was no way he could get what he needed now that he was out here. What was she thinking?

"Yes," he frowned, "there is a problem. I don't have diving equipment."

"Oh, don't worry about that. I have some suits on board Mike's boat. He always keeps spare equipment. You'll find everything you need on the boat."

Everything except experienced divers.

Brian rubbed his forehead, sighing now. "Can I talk to you Sadie" he asked, "in private?"

Carla's eyes grew wide as they left her sitting in the kitchen alone while they walked down the hall into another room to talk. "I can't do this job Sadie," he said, annoyed. "I'm not experience enough, nor do I have the manpower it takes to drag a 700 ft deep lake like Deep Bay. If he drowned, nobody's ever going to find him."

"You need to tell her that then."

"I thought you said she was reliable."

"She is, as far as I know. Look Brian. I'm sorry you came all the way up here for nothing. I assumed she filled you in on the major details when she talked to you on the phone."

"All she told me was her name and that her boyfriend was missing, that's all."

Silence filled the room then. Sadie shook her head and whispered, "That's it? Oh Brian, I'm very sorry. I'll pay for your trip up here. I didn't realize."

"No," Brian said, "It's not your fault. I'm just going to tell her I can't take the case, that's all."

The two of them came out of the room and headed for the kitchen. Carla was already making her way out the front door.

"Carla?" Sadie called after her, stopping her before she could go any further. "Where are you going?"

"I'm just going to get the boat ready."

"I can't take the case," Brian blurted out, hoping the woman wouldn't take it hard.

Carla started sobbing. "Please," she insisted. You have to. I'll pay you anything. Please!" The woman rushed over to Brian and pulled out a wad of bills from her pocket, stuffing them into Brian's hand with her long pink fingernails. "I have more. I'll pay you anything. Please! I need to find him."

Brian sighed, and looked at Sadie's sorry eyes. If he was going to take this case, it would be against his better judgement. "Fine," he mumbled, turning to Sadie. But I need some help then. Sadie? Could you come along?"

Sadie's eyes grew wide. "Me? I don't know how to scuba-dive?

"I do," a small cherub voice interrupted from the background.

Sadie turned to the teenage girl and took her by the hand to join in their discussion. "This is Dinah. She's a sponsored guest here."

"I use to be on a diving team at school," Dinah smiled.

"I didn't know that sweetheart," Sadie said, mothering her with hugs.

"When you grow up in Vancouver, you learn how to dive," Dinah said. "So, what do you want me to do?"

Brian wondered if it was wise to take a teenager out with him, but figured that's all the expertise he'd get way out here in the middle of nowhere. "Dinah, I want you to suit up with me and Carla. We're going to go down together. You do what I say and you follow me. Do you understand?"

"Cool," Dinah said.

"Sadie, I want you to come along too," he said, "for safety reasons."

"I can't leave my other guest," Sadie blurted out in a panic, "and besides, I don't like the water. I would really like to just stay here."

Brian eyeballed her, "I *need* you along," he whispered in her ear. "I don't want to go out there with two women I don't even know."

"What about my other guest. I can't leave her alone right now."

"Take her along."

Sadie gave him a strange glare and sighed, "Fine...Dinah, go tell Eunice she's going on a boat ride. I'll get some food together and meet you in the boat –but I hope you know I'm going to hate every minute of this."

"I know."

~~~~

The trail went cold shortly after following it last night. Instead, it led Pip to Reefers Island, an outcrop of rock formations the size of a small town on the east side of Deep Bay. You couldn't get back to land without swimming for miles, but it *was* possible...at least for a native Chipewyan man anyway.

For now, Pip would stay on the island, and see if he could pick up the trail again. The men he was working for would be alright by themselves for a while. He'd just tell them he heard the monster last night and took off after him by himself because they were passed out drunk.

On second thought, Pip scrapped that idea. He definitely wouldn't tell *that*, in fact, he wouldn't tell them anything. They still didn't seem very trustworthy. No, he'd take one more quick look around and then head back down to the cavern before they even noticed he was gone...but he had to hurry, the sun was already up.

As Pip dove down fifty feet from shore, swimming deep as he followed the passageway between two rocks, he found the entryway to the cavern. It was a familiar route for him ever since he found it here two years ago.

He'd been trailing the beast now for a while, seeing the devastation it could cause. That cruise boat that went down last year, reminded him of the murders that went on during the Shooting Star incident when he was just a kid. There was blood everywhere.

The monster didn't see him as he hid nearby, watching the horror. It was then that Pip finally got a good look at the thing and knew he never wanted to tackle such a beast.

It was ancient...pre-historic in a way, yet familiar at the same time. Pip thought it could just swim until he started following it. Then, as it crawled up on Reefers Island, he saw the scaly webbed feet that carried him into the forest.

Pip considered this piece of information very interesting at the time, though he told no one, not even the guys at the logging company where he worked. They told stories of the beast almost every night as they sat around the campfire, coming up with all sorts of false information.

It was Pip's secret. He enjoyed being the only one that knew. Not even Grandfather knew this bit of detail, though, even if he did, he wouldn't have remembered it. All he ever did now was sit in that nursing home rocking in his rocking chair. He'd been that way ever since his old friend Grayling died of a heart attack last year.

Pip sure missed *both* of them.

His brothers went south as soon as they could, both of them ending up in prison...just like Uncle Leon. But that was the past, and one thing Grayling taught him was never to dwell on the past.

He was all grown up now, living on his own in the old cabin, and already holding a job even if it was just casual. He'd fill in for someone if they were sick, log for a while until they came back, and do some guiding for the local tourists once in a while.

It was all he needed.

As Pip neared the place where he had left the men, he suddenly stopped and listened to the voices. *Great, they were already awake.*

"So where is he then?" Adam said sternly.

"I don't know man," Cutter said, "but I have a funny feeling Mike's right. I think the kid *is* on to us."

Pip's eyes grew wide. What was this all about?

"Of course, he's onto us," Mike said smugly. "Why do you think he took off?"

"But how does he know?" Adam questioned. "I didn't say anything. You guys didn't say anything. Carla doesn't even know."

"Trust me bud," Mike said. "He knows, that's why we have to find him, now stop yapping and get moving."

Pip jumped then and realized he had to get out of there. They were after him and he wasn't about to stick around to be caught. He knew they were up to no good right from the start. Grayling always told him to trust his gut. Why hadn't he listened?

Then, as Pip darted around a corner, his foot slipped sending crumbling pieces of gravel trickling down into the water below. Mike turned, saw him with his big beady eyes, and shouted to the others, "He's over here!"

Chapter 5

My back is *so* sore," Eunice complained for the umpteenth time. "We've been out here all day and we haven't even found one piece of evidence that this *stupid* woman and her *boyfriend* were even out here. For all we know, she made the whole thing up."

"She wouldn't make it up Eunice," Sadie said, trying to calm the woman down. "If it were *your*...man. You would want to keep looking."

"If it were *my* man, I wouldn't even bother."

Sadie sat there with her floppy green and yellow sun-hat and long sleeve shirt, listening to the woman's constant whining. It had been going on steady since the last time Brian and the girls checked in over and hour ago. She hoped they would come up soon; they were overdue about fifteen minutes already.

"And that's another thing," Eunice went on, "I didn't ask to come along on this little excursion, I'm nine months pregnant and I shouldn't even be out here."

Sadie almost choked on the Gravol pill she just popped in her mouth. "You're what?" she coughed, hoping she hadn't heard what she thought she heard.

Eunice played dumb. "*What?*"

Sadie tried not to get mad, but between the nausea and the glaring sun, she couldn't help but grit her teeth when she said, "you did *not* just tell me you're nine months pregnant."

"We'll...sort of."

"How can you be sort of nine months pregnant?"

"I...um, thought you knew."

"You told me you were six months along."

"Sorry."

Sadie suddenly stood up in the boat, and teetered toward the engine. "How do you start this thing? We're going home immediately, and then I'm calling your family or...I'll call your church and they can come pick you up."

"Wait, don't do that," Eunice begged. "I've given birth to four children, and I *know* this little guy isn't anywhere near ready yet. *Please*! I need more time."

"You don't have more time Eunice."

Sadie turned the key and revved the boat to life. She was responsible for this woman and there was no way she would allow her to be out on the water in her condition.

"We can't leave *them* down there Sadie."

"Right." What was she going to do? Perhaps she could run the woman back to the lodge and call her church, then drive back out to pick up Brian and the girls. But she had to wait, Brian was counting on her.

"You don't even know how to drive it."

Sadie took a deep breath, realizing she couldn't go anywhere. They would have to stay put for a little while longer. In the mean time, she intended to give this woman a crash course in Christianity 101. The soft method wasn't getting through to her and she had completely run out of time.

Lord help me to calm down and take this frustration from me.

"Okay," Sadie breathed, returning to her senses. "You had me going there for a bit, I'm not quite myself on this boat. I apologize. I just want to help you Eunice."

"I appreciate it, and I assure you I'm not having this baby *anytime* soon. Believe me. You can relax now."

Sadie leaned back in the driver seat and looked up into the sunny blue sky, inhaling through her nose and mouth. "Boy, you would think I was the one having this baby the way I'm breathing."

The two women began to giggle while the boat still idled in the deep water. The mood had definitely changed, Sadie was thankful. Things were looking up again, and the Gravol had taken her nausea completely away.

"I guess I'd better turn off the motor then," Sadie giggled with Eunice.

Fumbling around, Sadie couldn't seem to remember how she had turned the big cruising boat on. Was it with a key, or a lever? Then she recognized it. It was the big silver lever she saw Brian use the whole way out there.

She thrust it down with force, but instead of shutting it off, it sped backward, smashing hard against a jagged rock-cliff.

"Oh no!" Sadie cried. "What have I done?"

"I don't know," Eunice panicked, "but there's water coming in everywhere!"

~~~~

Brian heard something rumble above them as he and the two girls rose underwater toward the surface. He motioned for them to hurry up. If someone had started the boat, it wasn't a good thing. Sadie didn't even know how.

Luckily, the glowing sun made it easier for them to go up. All they had to do was follow the brightness…and the shadow of the boat at the top.

They'd been diving all day, checking in every hour, and still they hadn't found any clues as to where Carla's boyfriend Mike and the three men he had with him, had gone. If they were injured or dead, he would have found some evidence to support that, but there was nothing, not even the blood Carla said she saw yesterday. Maybe they were looking in the wrong spot.

Brian kicked his flippers hard, leaving the girls far behind him. Surely, he'd reach the surface soon. It didn't look that far away, but then again, he wasn't an experienced diver. Yes, he knew what he was doing, but he had only been trained for search and rescue through the police department and that was years ago. The only diving experience he had was in the North Saskatchewan River, rescuing a boy who had fallen in.

Deep Bay had a depth of around 700 ft. That was very deep for a lake, but because of the meteorite, it was much deeper than the other parts of Reindeer Lake. The North Saskatchewan River was nothing compared to this. He doubted they even dove down five hundred feet. It was impossible to reach the bottom although Dinah tried. She claimed she could make it with her ocean training, but he wasn't about to let her go. It was far too dangerous with the jagged rock formations he saw down there. He didn't know what he was going to do, just that they were done for the day. All he cared about now was reaching the surface as fast as he could.

When Brian popped his head above water, he slipped his goggles to his forehead and saw the devastation. There in the water, were the two women he left behind, wet as soaked rats, clinging to a half submerged boat. "What happened?" he shouted, swimming over to them, spitting out excess water from his mouth.

"We're sinking," Sadie shivered with a blue mouth.

"How?"

"She tried to drive the stupid thing," Eunice shouted in anger.

Brian sighed and looked around. Nothing but water filled the horizon except for a small outcrop of jagged rocks they had crashed against and an island in the distance.

Dinah and Carla rose to the surface then, shouting and waving their arms as they swam over to the wreck.

"My boat!" Carla shouted. "What happened to my boat?"

"It's sinking," Eunice blurted out. "What do you think?"

Dinah didn't say a word, she just tread water and waited beside Brian. The girl was more of a help then Carla was. He could use a kid like her right now.

"Dinah," he said, "grab the cooler and whatever you can from the boat before it goes all the way under. We only have a few minutes. Carla, I want you to get all the life preservers you can find, were going to have to swim our way to that island over there."

"Swim?" Eunice cried. "How am I supposed to swim with this big belly?"

"We'll help you."

By the time the boat was completely submerged, Brian and the four ladies were only a few feet away, hanging onto life preservers, with a train of belongings tied to each of them. The two orange coolers floated all by themselves with a little help from Brian. He tied them together, pulling them with one arm, using his other to help the pregnant one. "Don't strain yourself ma'am," he told Eunice. "Just try to use your arms and legs as little as possible. We'll get to the island even if it takes us twice as long as the others."

He couldn't imagine someone as pregnant as she was, making the swim by herself. He remembered Jenny big and pregnant like this. It wasn't fun. Jenny had developed heart problems with their first and the second was a high-risk pregnancy. That's why they decided against having any other children after Nathan. He hoped Eunice had a strong heart. She was going to need it.

"So how far along are you?" Brian asked.

Eunice wiped brown hair and water from her eyes. "Oh, this baby isn't ready to pop out yet. I always look this big. I don't know why. It's in the genes I guess."

"But you're not going to deliver it right now though…are you?"

"Now?" Eunice laughed. "Definitely not, though water-birthing *had* crossed my mind. They say it's a lot easier than a hospital delivery. Do you know anything about it?"

Brian shook his head, recognizing his cue to change the topic.

In the distance, he saw the three women make it to shore, glad they had found the ropes so they could tie their belongings together. The women ahead of him dragged the stuff on shore and waved at him to tell them they were all right.

Discarding the air tanks and their scuba gear wasn't exactly what he wanted to do but there was no way they could drag all this stuff with them, and take the air tanks too. He hoped they wouldn't need them, but he figured this was the end of the investigation anyway. He needed to get these women to safety now.

His only regret was forgetting his nine-millimetre in the lockbox on board the boat. With all the confusion, it completely slipped his mind. How could they grab just about everything else but the gun? It was a stupid mistake, one he hoped wouldn't cause him a life. He'd been in a situation like this before, and it didn't exactly thrill him.

"Are you okay Eunice," he asked the woman after listening to her huffing and puffing. He wished he hadn't insisted on her coming with them. Had he realized the potential danger, he never would have suggested it. He should have known better. It wasn't very professional at all. Why didn't he turn this case down like he wanted to?

"I'm fine," Eunice told him. "Stop worrying about me. I'm just carrying around seventy extra pound that's all. You can't expect me to be Gertrude Ederle."

"Who?"

"You know, the first American woman to swim across the English Channel."

"I didn't know that," Brian grinned, amazed at the woman's obvious education. "You must be a teacher or something."

"No, just educated. I was going to be a doctor you know."

"What happened?"

"Life," the woman sighed, kicking her legs suddenly. "What was that?"

"What?"

"There's something down there!"

Suddenly, as the woman screamed, she pulled away from Brian. "It bit my leg!"

Chapter 6

"So, tell us what you know then," Mike drilled Pip.

"I told you I don't know what you're talking about."

"I don't believe you?" Mike said flatly; ready to take another swing at Pip while Cutter and Adam held him down.

Pip felt as though his teeth were falling out. The blood he tasted in his mouth made him want to spit, but he didn't dare, not while he was being held down by these guys. Cutter was almost crushing him with his body weight and he could hardly breathe.

Adam yanked his arm and started twisting while Mike thrust the blade of his pocket knife hard against Pip's neck. "Okay, okay!" he moaned, afraid if he didn't say something, they really would kill him. He'd make it up if he had to.

"I knew it!" Cutter shouted, releasing his body weight from Pip. "You better tell us what you know. We don't have patience for dirty Indians like you."

When Mike released the knife from Pip's throat, he wiped the bloody skin, looked at it, then cupped it with his hand, taking a breath as he sat up. "There *are* a few things that I know," he said, watching the wide-eyed men as they listened.

"Just tell us what you know about the…"

"Shut up Cutter," Mike interrupted. "Just let him talk."

"This cave isn't just a cave," Pip said, playing with them, buying some time.

"I knew it," Cutter blurted out again. "The dirty Indian lied to us."

"Who told you?" Mike asked.

Pip dodged his head back and forth at the three of them, not knowing what to say next. All he knew was this cave was a passageway that led to Reefers Island. But why did these guys want to find it so badly? From day one, they had been asking him to take them to the caves.

"I said, who told you?" Mike shouted, grabbing Pips shirtfront, pulling him to his blonde-bearded face that looked like he hadn't had a shave in a long while.

"I –um…I figured it out."

"Then you should be able to take us there right now," Mike spit while he fumed. "Let's get going men. Pippi Longstocking is *finally* going to take us where we want to go, and if he doesn't…we'll let the monster have him."

Pip felt his body being pulled to his feet, while Mike attached his air tanks to his back as if he were a child. "There," Mike grinned, patting his shoulder. "You're all set Pippy. Now be a good boy and take us where we want to go."

As they shoved him forward to lead the way, Pip watched Cutter as he pulled out something from his bag. It wasn't just the camera, he always had that with him. It was something else, something that looked like…*Plastic explosives?!*

What were they doing with explosives?

~~~~~

Sadie stood there not knowing what to do. She couldn't swim, and taking that life preserver out there again didn't seem like a good idea. By the time she would reach Brian and Eunice, *she'd* be the one they had to save.

Before Sadie even had time to think, Dinah was on her way back into the water. Whatever the problem was with Eunice, her screaming alarmed her. "What is it?" she shouted to them, but they couldn't hear her.

Carla sat on a rock beside her with her hands cupped to her mouth and nose, sobbing softly as she watched and listened. Sadie sat down on a slimy grey rock as well and put her arm around the woman. At least she could do *that*.

What were they going to do?

Within minutes, Brian and Dinah brought Eunice to shore. She seemed much calmer and apparently okay except for her leg.

Sadie and Carla helped Eunice out of the water. She limped as they helped her sit down. Brian staggered out of the water breathing hard. "We just about didn't make it," he said gasping for air. "Something tried to pull Eunice under. If it hadn't been for Dinah, I really think we would have drowned."

That's my butterfly. "Are you all right Dinah?" Sadie asked, holding the teenager's cheeks, and then drawing her in for a long hug.

"I'm fine," Dinah said, squirming from Sadie's grip, "but Eunice *isn't*. Something bit her leg."

They both rushed over to Eunice, sitting there in the sand, big belly bulging against her clinging wet sundress and bare legs. It was apparent that something definitely had bitten her. Blood trickled down her right ankle.

"What was it?" Sadie asked, bending down to look at the woman's ankle.

"It was probably just a fish," Carla scoffed, sulking on her rock, disinterested in the situation with Eunice. Sadie wondered if it was because of their run-in last night, but she hoped it wasn't.

"It could have been just about anything," Brian said, kneeling to see the wound. "Stingrays, snakes, bugs, and yes...even fish...but whatever it was, it had to be big. It was pulling Eunice so hard, I couldn't grab her."

"Look," Eunice moaned, "It had it's teeth around my whole foot. See, there are teeth marks on both sides of my ankles."

Sadie and Dinah bent over Brian's shoulder to take a look. "Cool," Dinah said, "it kind of looks like a vampire bite...I mean, it's not really cool, actually it's freaky but you know what I mean. I'm glad you're okay Eunice."

"Hand me that first aid kit," Brian said, "I'll fix up the wound for you and then we have to find some place to spend the night. We're losing the sun already."

As Brian disinfected Eunice's wound and bandaged it up, Sadie watched Carla still sitting there pouting. It was obvious the woman was upset and needed someone to talk to. She had better go over and talk to her.

"Carla?" Sadie said softly as she sat down next to her. "Are you okay?"

At first all Carla did was shrug her off, but Sadie kept on trying to converse. "Are you upset because we're all paying attention to Eunice?"

The woman tried to smile but her tears wouldn't let her. "No," she sniffled, wiping her nose with her black scuba-diving suit. "I don't care about *her*."

I know that already. "Then what?"

~~~~

What do you think bush-woman! She wanted to scream. Carla's magnificent boat had been completely destroyed. That thing cost her a great deal, and not just in money. It was a gift she had given Mike for their one-month anniversary. It meant a lot to her even though Mike didn't really care.

Well, she shouldn't say he didn't care. He cared all right. He cared so much about it that he begged her for it. "I need it babe, *please!*" he said. "Me and the boys will take you on one *whopping* treasure hunt. It'll be fun."

So, being the sucker that she was, she fell for it. *Anything to please a man.* And she had more money than she could shake a stick at, *so,* –Why not? It didn't occur to her at the time that he was using her. Well, she couldn't honestly say that either. She *knew* –but she didn't care. All she wanted was to be loved. She'd pay anything for that.

And now the boat was gone and so was Mike. Was it a coincidence, or punishment for the sins she had done?

When her father died and left her his entire estate shortly after she and John tied the knot, the money came in handy. They paid off all their debts and bought a home in Beverly Hills. Her father would have been happy; they bought one right next to Ace Anderson's mansion, the star of Action Ten. Carla even got to know him pretty well –in more ways than one.

But now, all that money seemed useless. It didn't buy her love, it didn't buy her happiness. She figured it was the only reason John didn't follow through with all his divorce threats. Money was a good friend –to everyone except for Carla.

Even after she'd bought Mike all that equipment for his treasure hunt, she still felt like he didn't really love her. She paid for all the shipping costs for the boat and supplies, all the way from California to Northern Canada, spending a fortune. Paid for the cost of the lodge, two weeks stay in advance, and plane fare for Cutter and Adam as well as herself and Mike. She even paid for a guide. And what for? *Nothing*.

Not even a private investigator could find them now. What did they do, skip off with a hundred grand worth of drilling equipment? *Big deal*. It didn't make sense.

Chapter 7

The bars of his prison cell locked simultaneously for the last time.

Anthony could hear the usual noise that wafted through the penitentiary after lights went out, disturbing as it was. But he learned to get use to it. Fifteen years in the slammer numbed him to a lot of things.

If he could only get through tomorrow, the last day of his sentence, without incident, he would be a free man, able to start life with a clean slate, if that were even possible after all this time.

Bell told him it would be tough, but she always reassured him with a Bible verse that seemed to give him hope. She led the Bible study with her team singing in the background, preaching like nobody's business.

At first Anthony thought she was nuts when she and her *prison ministry team* came to visit last year. She told him that God loved him and cared about what happened to him. It immediately turned him off, just like all the other churchy people that tried to convert the cons.

Then, Bell said something different that changed his thinking. "If you need a good lawyer, I can get you one for free," she said. "He's got a good reputation and his record is over the top —and when you're in front of the judge, he'll fight to the death for you. He'll even fight for a *not guilty* plea even if you did the crime. Now doesn't that sound like a good offer?"

Anthony still remembered that conversation, smiling as it continued through his mind. "How do I hire this lawyer?" he asked her.

"All you have to do is listen to me for a half hour."

Then she told him the story of Jesus. After that, she just kept coming every afternoon. He got to a point where he looked forward to her visits. Then one day, he bowed his head to pray with her and her team. It was like magic. He felt like a million pins were pricking into his skin, but it didn't hurt. He tingled all over until the tears started running down his ruddy face against his will.

It was truly amazing.

Now, after being a believer for ten year, he held a Bible study of his own with the other inmates, mostly the new ones because he wanted to reach them first before the wolves did. The lifers were vicious like that. They got to *him* the first day coming to this joint and he was determined to protect the lambs like Jesus did.

They nicknamed him "Shepherd" but he didn't mind. Most of the guys left him alone, but sometimes he took a beating on behalf of a newbie, especially from *Ice*, one of the roughest guys in there.

Last year Ice puzzled him though. He had signed up for re-education classes, sitting right next to him most of the time. Shepherd thought, either this guy found the Lord, or, he had changed his life *somehow*. Taking all those Geology courses sure didn't suit a tough ex-gang member.

It wasn't until lately that Shepherd overheard a conversation between Ice and a buddy that had come to visit. "I'm getting out soon," Ice told his visitor, confusing Anthony because he knew he had many years left to his sentence.

"Good, because I have everything set to go," the overweight man on the chair beside him spoke in a whisper. "We found a benefactor, and she's funding the whole thing for us."

"Perfect," Ice said, "I gave you guys the details so you should be able to start the job before I get there. And make sure you actually get some work done, because if I show up and you haven't done a thing, you know what's going to happen."

"Oh, we will," the fat man said.

"And keep it quiet," Ice whispered. "I'm not exactly a free man –yet."

Just then, Ice looked up and noticed Shepherd listening in. His heart skipped a beat when he realized Ice was directing a string of swear words at him. "Mind your own business Shepherd," he said, adding another four-letter word to his scolding. Shepherd immediately pushed his chair away from the table, screeching the chair-legs against the floor as he did it. "No problem," he said, knocking the chair over, raising his hands as if the man had a gun to him. In different circumstances, he knew that Ice wouldn't hesitate to shoot him.

Shaking the memory from his mind, Shepherd lay on his cot unable to sleep. He wondered why Ice hadn't come after him today. It was as if he deliberately left him alone because he was leaving tomorrow. But he knew him better than that. The guy had it out for him the minute he eavesdropped on that conversation.

Lord, help me live to see freedom tomorrow.

Chapter 8

Brian was a good man. Sadie could see it in the way he took care of them, making sure the fire continued to blaze, fetching anything that would burn. The makeshift shelter he built out of evergreen branches even impressed her.

Jenny was a lucky woman.

Sometimes as content as she felt being single, she couldn't help but long for a provider like Brian. What would her life be like if she had a soul mate to share her life with? It was a question that popped up now and then, especially on moonlit nights with stars twinkling in the sky like right now.

Snap out of it Sadie.

No, she swallowed hard and told herself that she wasn't missing out by not being married. She told herself that having a man around wouldn't make a difference even if he *could* protect her –but she sure was glad he was protecting them all now.

As Sadie, Eunice, Carla, and Dinah all huddled around the fire as Brian flopped another log on the fire, she wondered what next. "So, what are we going to do from here?" she asked her old friend.

"Well," Brian sat down with them and sighed. "Tomorrow morning, I'll swim back to land, hike my way to the lodge and call for help. We don't have any other choices here ladies."

"But that will take a while."

"I know Sadie, but we've run out of options."

"I got an Idea," Dinah chided. "How about I go with you. I'm a good hiker."

With a frown, Sadie patted Dinah's helpful head and told her no. "You need to stay here with us sweetie. It's not safe."

"I'm not a *baby* Sadie."

"I know you're not, but…"

Brian grinned and kicked his shoe at the fire interrupting them both. "Okay," he said. "How about this. Since you want to help, you can keep the fire going here. It's an important job you know. There are a lot of bush planes that fly by. Someone might see the smoke and set down their plane. *You* can be the hero then."

"*Right!*" Dinah smiled, "Why do I get the feeling that you're patronizing me?"

The group fell quiet then. Sadie wanted to say something to the girl, but she didn't know what to say. Then Brian started laughing.

"What's so funny?" Dinah blurted out.

"I'm sorry," he said. "It's just that my son Patrick said the same thing to me when he wanted to go snowboarding. I told him no, that it was too dangerous, but he said what you said. I know it's not exactly the same thing, but it *is* kind of funny. He thought he knew better than me, told me he wasn't a baby and that he could do it no problem. Do you want to know what happened?"

"Do I have a choice?" Dinah asked rolling her eyes.

"No," Brian grinned. "So, listen. Patrick continued to beg me to let him go snowboarding until I was so sick of his asking that I caved. Regrettably, I let him go, against my better judgment, and he came back with a broken arm, broken leg, and a concussion. He spent a week in the hospital and wished he would have listened to me."

"That's not going to happen to me," Dinah argued.

"Listen to him dear," Sadie tried to butt in. "He knows what he's talking about. He got lost in the bush up here five years ago. He knows what dangers lurk out there. Don't you Brian?"

"All too well," Brian said growing more serious now. "People died."

A wolf howled in the distance just then, making Dinah jump. "Okay," she groaned. "You made your point. I'm sitting by you then."

As Dinah got up to sit beside Brian, Sadie gazed over at Carla and Eunice, faces lighted by the flickering fire. She wondered if she should try to resume her Bible study. These two women needed to hear God's word even if they were stranded in the middle of nowhere –but she didn't know how to breach the topic. It wasn't exactly the ideal time.

"How about one of your Bible studies Sadie," Brian piped up all of a sudden.

Thank you, Lord.

Eunice moaned, "No way! Not if Miss Foot Loose and Fancy Free gets to talk."

"Why do you hate me so much?" Carla fumed. "You don't even know me. I'm a nice person you know. Everybody says so."

"Am I missing something?" Brian interrupted their squabble.

"Just last nights Bible study, that's all," Sadie sighed. "Look, lets pick a different topic just so everyone is happy. What would *you* like me to teach on Brian?"

"Oh...I don't know," Brian pondered, "How about...Christian living?"

Great. For some reason, Sadie just knew it was going to be a *long* night now.

~~~

Pip stumbled along as he led the three men to the center of the cave. He didn't know where else to lead them. If he took them all the way to the end where the opening was, he'd be killed for sure. They would figure out that he *didn't* know what they were talking about.

How could he get himself out of this mess?

He knew it must be after dark by now, but there was no way of knowing. Not that it mattered much, but the monster would eventually want to come back home to it's cave. And this was definitely it's cave.

"So, are we there yet?" Cutter blurted out, huffing and puffing, obviously tired out. "I can't go any further without taking a break."

"If you'd lose fifty pounds bro, you might actually be able to do it," Mike heckled.

"Shut up big shot," Cutter snapped back. "You think I like being fat?"

"If you stop eating bon-bons all the time," Mike teased, "you might actually lose weight. Try eating tofu like I do."

"No way! And I don't eat bon-bons either!" Cutter fumed, "I can't afford the *healthy* foods Mr. Geologist. That stuff costs money which I don't have, remember?"

"Oh, and you think just because I'm a geologist I have money?"

"More than me."

"Not no more," Adam laughed. "Don't you remember the fraud charges? Wasn't it embezzlement too *Mr. Geologist*?"

"Oh, shut up you guys. I might have lost my job and my money but I'm still a geologist, unlike you guys."

"Yah," Cutter teased, "a geologist that needs an old lady to pay for everything."

"That's enough Cutter!" Mike yelled now, echoing throughout the cave, "I'm sick of your stupid jokes. If you don't shut up, I'm going to *shut* you up."

Pip found this conversation very interesting. He had learned a lot by their little outburst. Mike was a geologist and the other two were his helpers.

So, they wanted to do some mining did they?

Pip decided to tell them that this was the spot. It was the center point of the cave and beautiful with its outcrop of different rocks. To a geologist, this place had to mean something. Exactly what, Pip didn't quite know yet.

"This is it," Pip said cringing, wondering if he was doing the right thing. A mistake now could cost him his life.

"Great," Mike answered, throwing Pip a pack of explosives. "You're in with us now Pippi Longstocking. Help us set the C4 charges. We're going to blow it."

~~~~

Brian couldn't figure out what was going on with Eunice and Carla, they had been arguing for the last hour and it was beginning to confuse even him.

"I still think you can be a Christian and not go to church," Carla disputed her case.

"Technically yes," Sadie told her, "but why would you want to be out in the world alone like a lost little sheep? The wolves will eat you up before you even see them coming. We're safer in numbers you know."

Brian knew she was right. If it hadn't been for the people in his church, he and Jenny wouldn't know a thing about Christianity. They took them under their wings and taught them the do's and don'ts according to God's laws. He couldn't imagine having to decipher the Bible all by himself. People get all sorts of things twisted when they do that. Everyone needs a qualified teacher like a pastor to guide them, and you usually find them in church. Not only that, when we don't go to church, we lose fellowship with our brothers and sisters in Christ which causes a breakdown in communication just like family members that live so far apart.

"What about you Sadie?" Carla went on. "Where do you go to church out here in the middle of the bush?"

Brian's eyes beamed, waiting for Sadie's answer. She usually had a good one.

"Well you can obviously guess where I go to church," Sadie told her with a matter of fact tone. "It's not possible to go to a traditional church out here. There is none. I fellowship with other believers by phone, by E-mail, by letter. I keep in contact with each church that sponsors a guest here. I hold my own Bible studies and a church service on Sundays with the guests I have, and I have to answer to the higher ups like the church board that sponsors the lodge. They keep me in line so I don't misguide anyone."

Brian heard the loons on the lake as soon as the discussion fell silent. Sadie said a mouthful, just like he knew she would, and that obviously shut Carla up.

"I don't get your problem Carla," Eunice piped up all of a sudden after being quiet for some time. "You don't go to church, yet you profess to be a

Christian. You fool around on your husband, yet you think that's okay. What part of God's laws are unclear to you?"

"Like I said before," Carla cleared her throat, "I know I have problems, but God isn't just going to turn his back on me because of them. *You* obviously have problems. Look at you. You're about to pop that kid out and you're at a Christian retreat. Why? What kind of skeletons do you have in *your* closet?"

Brain hated this. Listening to women squabble wasn't exactly his thing. He'd always try to sneak off whenever Jenny and her mother got into an argument like this. Trouble was, he couldn't exactly leave these women alone, he'd have to wait it out.

"Now ladies," Sadie interrupted the women. "This isn't the way to discuss Christian living. The Bible says in 2 Timothy 2:24: "A servant of the Lord must not quarrel but be gentle to all, able to teach, patient.""

It was an answer that didn't shock Brian, though it seemed to shock the rest of them. He knew Sadie's head was full of memorized Bible verses. She was in fact, a good teacher, and she didn't need a Bible in her hand to do it. That's why they hired her to run Shining Star Lodge. These women didn't know who they were dealing with, but Brian knew.

"I don't care," Eunice went on, fidgeting, shifting her weight as she sat. Obviously, she was uncomfortable. "I never have been one to control my emotions. Besides, that Bible verse is a bit unrealistic. How are we supposed to be gentle to *all*? It's impossible. Why would God demand us to do something so impossible?"

"God demands obedience," Sadie gently spoke.

"Oh, so you're saying I'm supposed to do the impossible?"

"You're supposed to *try* to follow his ways."

Eunice started crying then, frustrating Brian. He never knew what to do when a woman cried. It was awkward. Emotions were not his thing.

"I HAVE TRIED!" Eunice screamed through tears. "I've tried for fifteen years. I love my kids. Am I supposed to turn my back on them so I can obey God? Does he really want me to choose?"

Then Eunice broke down completely, bawling like a child, hiccups and all. She cried so loudly it echoed through the dark trees around them.

"I HATE YOU GOD! Eunice shouted against the night.

Nobody said a thing until Carla decided to stand up, walk over to Eunice, and put her arm around the poor bawling woman. It was out of character from what Brian could see, but it was nice.

"I don't know what's upsetting you honey," Carla tried to consol her, draping her arm around Eunice. "But...I *am* sorry I upset you. I didn't mean to."

Eunice just shook as she sobbed in Carla's arms.

Sadie sat on the other side of Eunice, hugging her with one arm as she prayed for her. During her prayer, Brian finally put it all together. The woman was fighting for her soul, torn between a life of mistakes, living with the repercussions, unable to get out of the bondage of sin Satan had tricked her into.

The prayer said it all.

Chapter 9

Shepherd hadn't realized it then, but Ice must have followed him all the way from the P.A pen. He didn't know how he got out, but that didn't matter, the fact was he had him at gunpoint and forced him on the floatplane.

He sure was a free man all right. After fifteen years of lock-up, the day he's released he gets kidnapped. How is that possible? He knew freedom was a joke.

Why did he have to eavesdrop on Ice anyway? If he had minded his own business, he wouldn't be in this mess.

Ice had made him charter a floatplane and pay for it with a stolen credit card. After they had been flying for a while, he started arguing and punching him as they flew above water. But he fought back, hard, maybe a little too hard. He lost his balance, falling right out of the plane into the icy cold water. Luckily, it was very deep water.

One good thing about falling out of the plane was that he had gotten away from Ice, but swimming to shore was an ordeal, especially after a fish took a good nip at his leg while he was swimming. It caught him off guard in the dark water, and nearly pulled him under.

Now as he crawled up on the solid rock formations that edged the island, he found himself on, he realized the dawn was just rising through the trees…and he could see he had landed in some kind of paradise.

~~~~

Morning broke with the sound of Eunice moaning.

At first Sadie thought the woman was in labour, but after she ran to her side, she realized it was something else. The bite mark around her foot was infected.

"I don't understand it," Brian sighed, observing the bite. "I disinfected the wound before I bandaged it up. It shouldn't be this bad."

Sadie observed the open wound. What originated as bite marks now appeared more like large gaping holes through the woman's ankle. Green and yellow puss oozed from the wound unlike anything she had ever seen before.

"Brian," Sadie whispered, "Can I talk to you in private?" She motioned for him to follow her out of earshot from the others.

As Dinah and Carla knelt beside Eunice, trying to calm her down, Sadie led Brian to a crop of trees near the edge of the island. "This is bad," Sadie said as she turned to him when they were far enough away. "You have to get some help."

"I know," Brian agreed. "I wanted to take off as soon as possible, but I'm not sure swimming is the best way to go with that *thing* in the water."

"Then what are we going to do?"

Brian rubbed his head, and looked around. "Let's just play it by ear. We'll take care of Eunice first, make sure she's okay, then we'll build a fire again. I thought I heard a floatplane in the air earlier. Hopefully it'll pass by again. If it's in the area, it should see our smoke."

"Hopefully," Sadie fretted, turning her head to a strange sound. "Did you hear that?"

"Yes, I did," Brian answered her with alarm in his voice, "It's coming from over there."

Brian led Sadie by the hand as they both took off away from camp, across the jagged shoreline toward the water. A man was sitting on a rock, calling for help.

~~~~

All the C4 was in place.

Pip had come up with a plan to convince them to wait until morning to set up the plastic explosives, that way he could secretly sneak off in the middle of the night when they were asleep, like the last time.

But it didn't work.

They tied him to a huge boulder until morning.

"Okay men," Mike announced. "This is the plan. Before we let her blow, I want all of you to know exactly what we're looking for. I want diamonds boys…and you know who else wants diamonds. If we don't have any by the time *he* gets here, you're going to wish the Loch Ness Monster was your best friend."

Now Pip knew, and it all sounded vaguely familiar.

"But how do we know what they look like?" Cutter asked. "I'm not use to raw diamonds. I wouldn't know one if my life depended on it. I'm use to cutting polished rocks that someone else cut already."

Diamond cutter.

Now it was all making sense to Pip.

"Look Cutter," Mike started talking slowly. "This is the way it is. I'm looking for impact-crater diamonds from the meteorite that struck this bay. They're opaque diamonds. You know…impervious?"

Cutter looked dumbfounded. "What?"

"He has an eighth-grade education Mike, give him a break," Adam laughed. "You have to talk in *kindergarten* language."

Cutter punched Adams arm. "Shut up freak."

"Okay look," Mike sighed. "Impervious means non-transparent. Were looking for dark rocks that won't allow light to shine through them. Rough diamonds aren't going to look clear and shiny, they're dark and appear to be greasy, so watch for that."

While they were talking Pip tried to think of a way to get away from them. Maybe he could run when the explosion hit. He knew his way around the cave and they didn't.

"And Pippi Longstocking," Mike added, grabbing him by the scruff of the neck. "You're coming with me."

"What?" Adam complained. "Where are *you* going?"

"Pippy's going to take me topside to Reefers Island," Mike told him. "And yes, Pippy, I know about Reefers Island. I just didn't know how to find it until you found the cave for me. You were supposed to take us here a week ago."

That's when you said you were hunting the monster.

"But why are you going up there, Mike?" Cutter asked. "I thought you were going to help us collect the rough diamonds. How will we know were collecting the right thing?" Mike shook his head. "Aside from the fact that I already told you," Mike said, annoyed, "Adam knows what to look for. Just ask him. I want to look for micro diamonds, they're less than 1mm across. I have the equipment for it, and I'm the only one that knows how to use it. Most people don't even know they exist. They're generally younger than Kimberlitic diamonds, relics actually…graphite relics of larger diamonds. But then, you don't understand a word I'm saying anyway Cutter, so why am I wasting my breath?"

Mike grabbed his equipment bag and started off with Pip. He was glad he was getting out of there. Once he reached the water, he could escape for sure.

"When will you be back bro?" Adam shouted after them.

"In a while. Just give me an hour before you blow the C4. And make sure you're in a safe place before you do it. I don't want to come back to a mess. Got it?"

If Mike thought he wasn't going to have a mess with all the C4 charges they set, he was crazy. Pip wasn't as educated as Mike, but he at least knew what would happen when an underwater cave explodes.

These guys were nuts.

Chapter 10

The strange man told them his boat sunk too and he was stranded like them. He looked rough unshaven and dirty and had large cross tattoos that stood out on his huge forearms. He actually appealed to Carla, but she didn't say anything. The man had taken a shining to Sadie instead. Who knows why?

"So, you just got out?" Sadie asked him again.

"Yes," the man called Shepherd told them for the umpteenth time. Carla was getting a little sick of talking about his recent prison release after fifteen years. She couldn't imagine surviving in a place like that.

Why couldn't they concentrate on Eunice. She was getting worse. Her foot now looked swollen and green.

"Are you okay Eunice?" Carla smiled as she sat down beside the woman laying in the makeshift hut Brian had made for them.

Eunice slowly sat up, appearing sweaty and serious. She looked around as if checking to see if anyone was listening in on their conversation. "I appreciated your comfort last night when I lost it, and I just wanted you to know that I trust you now. You and I are cut from the same cloth even though we've done nothing but fight. I'm sorry about that. I really do have a reason for my emotional outbursts. That's why I wanted to talk to you. Can I tell you a secret?" she whispered.

"I guess so," Carla said, bringing her ear closer to the whispering woman.

"Don't tell anybody…but I'm in labour."

~~~~~

Shepherd found these people to be a pleasant surprise. The Lord obviously had a sense of humour for him to meet up with them the way he did.

He told both Brian and Sadie how he had found the Lord in prison and how he had taught a Bible study in there.

It was Sadie he found most fascinating. She was doing the same thing as he was, but on the outside. In fact, she was a breath of fresh air with her natural looks and loving personality. She reminded him of a younger version of Bell.

As the fire roared in front of them, Shepherd noticed the young one they called Dinah, slip away to gather twigs, Carla and the pregnant one were off in the shelter visiting about something. He wasn't quite sure whether they were believers, but Brian and Sadie defiantly were. He couldn't remember the last time he was able to talk so freely about the Lord. He enjoyed it and took every opportunity.

"So," he said, "do you think that the Lord is watching our backs right now?"

"Most definitely," Sadie smiled.

"What about you Brian?"

"Sure, but it makes me scratch my head a bit?"

Sadie pouted, looking guilty. "What Brian probably means is that I'm to blame," she cringed. "You see, I drove the boat into a rock and now were here. It's my fault, and now we have to suffer the consequences. It's like jumping in front of a train. God is always with us, but when we deliberately do something stupid, like jumping in front of a train…a natural reaction occurs –we get hit."

"But God still has our backs, right?" Shepherd insisted.

"Yes," Sadie said as she hung her head and then looked up at Brian and back to Shepherd. "He still has our backs, but if we get squashed from a train *we* jumped in front of, he's going to have to set the bones and mend us up like a doctor. Picking up the pieces of our own stupidity isn't so easy, it's painful. People tend to cringe at the thought of pain."

Brian interrupted. "She's smart, isn't she?"

"Yes, she is."

Shepherd could use a woman like her, she makes the Bible sound simple. The inmates in his own Bible study had so many questions he didn't know how to answer, or if he did, he couldn't seem to get them to understand.

"I'm not all that smart gentlemen," Sadie answered back immediately. "I put us all in danger with my stupidity. I didn't even know how to drive a boat. It's the same thing as jumping in front of a train. Now Eunice is hurt and it's all my fault."

"It's not your fault Sadie," Brian reassured her. "Nobody blames you…and it's not the same thing as jumping in front of a train."

Shepherd looked over at the pregnant woman. "What's wrong with Eunice?"

They filled him in about the infected bite, and her delicate condition that he already gathered from the size of her belly. Then he reached down and pulled up his own pant-leg showing them the fish-bite he had received. "Does it look anything like this?" Shepherd asked them, sticking out his leg, revealing two red holes on either side of his limb that had stopped bleeding already.

Brian and Sadie grew quiet. The serious alarming look they gave him said it all.

~~~~

As they neared the opening, Pip heard something from behind. If he wasn't mistaken, it was Cutter and Adam. *What were they doing here?*

"Wait up Mike," Adam shouted startling Mike. He obviously hadn't heard them until now. Pip knew something was following them a half-hour ago, but he thought it was the monster.

"What are you two doing here?" Mike spun around in alarm. "I told you two to stay down there. And why is Cutter limping?

Pip perched on a rock to listen and wait. He couldn't exactly sneak off now.

"That's the thing Mike," Adam went on to explain, "I'm trying to tell you."

Adam helped Cutter ease to a sitting position while the big man moaned and babied his foot.

"Cutter was sitting on the edge of a rock while I set the charges. Then before I knew it, he was in the water —said something pulled him in."

"Something grabbed my foot Mike," Cutter moaned in a panic. "Seriously…if Adam hadn't been there to pull me out, that thing would have eaten me alive."

Mike stood there with his hands on his hips grinning as if he didn't believe a word they said. "Oh, come on," he laughed, "don't tell me the monster got you. Let me see the foot."

Cutter had on a pair of blue and black water shoes and stuck out his foot for them to see. Pip inched closer so he could see as well. Blood ran down his leg from two holes on either side of his ankle. If the monster had done this, it was being merciful. Pip saw the carnage that thing was capable of, and this was peanuts compare to that.

"Oh, that's nothing," Mike teased the fat man, "I've had shark bites bigger than that when I did some diving in the south pacific last year and *I* survived. Want to see my scars?"

"It *really* hurts Mike," Cutter moaned.

Mike pounded his fist on a rock, getting angry now. "I don't care! You two were supposed to stay back and set the explosives off."

"Oh, that's all taken care of," Adam interrupted. "We'll go back down tomorrow, after the C4 explodes. Cutter will be fine by then."

"You didn't put *all* the C4 on the same timer, did you?"

"Yup, I told you it would work," Adam grinned, looking at his watch. "It should go off in exactly…five minutes."

"You idiot!" Mike screamed. "I told you it *wouldn't* work. You know why Adam? Because we'd blow ourselves up. I told you that yesterday. You were *supposed* to set one small charge off at a time for safety, no matter what."

"I can go back."

"No, you can't!" Mike fumed. "You don't have enough time. Just grab fatso and let's get the heck out of here before the whole thing blows."

Chapter 11

How could she keep it a secret?

If Eunice didn't want anyone to know she was in labour, she was crazy. All you had to do was look at her and know something was up. But then, Sadie and Dinah had never had any children. Carla supposed Eunice would be able to fool them into thinking it was her foot that was causing her the pain.

Carla knew that sooner or later the others would catch on. She couldn't hide it for long, in fact, she wondered how she could hide it at all. For someone who wasn't good at hiding her emotions, she was doing a pretty good job.

Giving birth wasn't an easy thing, Carla knew that first hand. Each labour she went through, she screamed so loudly she lost her voice. Eunice was as quiet as a mouse.

"Are you sure you don't want me to say anything?" Carla asked her after returning with some food she had taken from one of the coolers.

Eunice blew air out of her mouth and said nothing until a contraction passed. "Whew, that was a big one," Eunice said, trying to regain her composure. "I don't want you to say *anything*. Promise me."

Carla didn't know how she could promise the woman. First, she hardly knew her, and secondly, it wasn't safe to hide something like this.

"I can't promise," Carla whispered. "But I'll do my best to keep it quiet for now."

"Good enough. Now help me up will you. My butts getting sore. Maybe you could take me for a walk. Brian made these crutches for me."

Are you nuts woman?

"No!" Carla snapped back, "definitely not, not in your condition."

Eunice shushed her and looked around. "Don't talk so loud, someone will hear you. Just help me up. My contractions are so far apart, there's no danger. My water hasn't even broken yet...and Brian bandaged my foot pretty good so I should be able to get around with some help."

Carla rolled her eyes and gave the bulging woman a hand up. "I'm not taking you far, so don't expect a tour of the island."

"Just take me through those trees. They look so beautiful."

"Fine," she said, "but I have to tell the others where were going."

As Carla helped Eunice hop-shuffle, she yelled back at the others sitting around the roaring fire. "I'm taking Eunice for a walk. We won't be gone long."

Sadie bent backward to look at them and shouted, "keep an eye out for Dinah while you're at it. She's been gone a while."

Carla and Eunice agreed, and hobbled down a rocky pathway toward a stately crop of dark green jack pines that stood boldly against the grey moss-covered rocks that protruded from the scanty soil.

"Do you know there's a myth about this place?" Eunice said as she struggled to move. "They say a monster lives in Deep Bay. Do you believe in that kind of stuff?"

"In what?"

"Monsters."

Carla cringed as she looked up into the morning sun. "I don't know...Mike does, but I don't really think I do."

"Well I do. I think that's what bit my foot."

"Oh Eunice –I don't think so."

"Well, it makes perfect sense. I think something evil has been after me for quite some time. When I first met Zack, my common-law husband, I could feel it even then. Seriously, you wouldn't believe the things that have happened to me since then."

Carla tried to humour the woman. "Like what?"

"When I first met him fifteen years ago, Zack pretended to be a believer. I met him at a church retreat. Whenever I was around him, I got this sick feeling in my stomach. I tried to stay away from him, but I couldn't. He followed me around like a stalker. Sometimes I even thought he was."

"What did you do?"

"I slept with him."

"What?" Carla's eyes bulged out. "You and I *are* cut from the same cloth."

"I didn't mean too," Eunice stopped for a moment as another contraction hit. This time it brought tears to her eyes, but she still didn't make a sound. When it was over, she continued on with her conversation as if nothing happened at all."

Now that's an acquired skill.

"Anyway," Eunice continued, looking up at the huge trees as they hobbled by. "I didn't mean to sleep with him. I don't know what happened, he was like a drug –a bad drug I couldn't shake. I still got the sick feeling every time I was around him, but after a while I figured out it was morning sickness."

"No!"

"Yes," she frowned, "I was only twenty-one and going to college. I dropped out and then my parents and my church disowned me. Zack never did though, that's one thing I respect him for. He and I moved in together. But you know what, the whole time, I felt like I was betraying someone."

"God?"

"You got that right," Eunice said, stopping again, "but I didn't know it then. I kept on living the way I wanted to even though Zack frightened me to death. He always said he was Catholic, but the meetings he would go to didn't sound like it. I still think he's into witchcraft, but I can't prove it."

"That's awful," Carla gasped. "What did you do?"

"We had more kids together even though he refused to marry me. Isn't that crazy? You'd think I'd learn. I still kept going to church though. I'd cry at the alter every Sunday and nobody knew why."

"I go to a different church now, and they try to help...but nothing *ever* helps. I still have bad things happen to me."

"What kind of bad things?"

"Accidents, sicknesses, and...I lost two babies."

Carla couldn't imagine that kind of pain. "You mean miscarriages?"

"No, I mean, *literally*. I lost them. One evening I came home early from Bible study and Christa was missing. She was only a toddler. Zack said she must have wandered off. I had my doubts, but he was Zack –smooth as ice. He couldn't have had anything to do with it, right? Anyway, there was this big investigation, but nobody ever found Christa. She vanished from our home without a trace."

Carla felt sorry for the woman. Tears streamed down her face as she watched her go through another contraction. They were coming more regularly now.

"We better go back," Carla insisted after the contraction had subsided.

"No!" Eunice said rather abruptly. "I need to tell you this."

Why she felt burdened to tell her all this, was beyond her. She barely knew the woman, though, she must admit, she was curious to hear more.

"Two years ago," Eunice went on, "it happened again. This time, I came home from a night of Bible study again, and Douglas was missing. He was my baby, only six months old. I was leery about leaving him with Zach in the first place. I should have listened to my gut, but Zach insisted. When I came home, there was no baby in the crib, and Zack didn't have the slightest idea what I was talking about. He said I took Douglas to Bible study with *me*."

"No! You didn't let him get away with it, did you?"

"No, I certainly did not. I phoned the sheriff, but he didn't do anything. No investigation, no nothing. What kind of sheriff doesn't send out a search party for a missing child? Really!"

"What did you do?"

"I found out that the sheriff belonged to the same cult as Zack, and that told me everything I needed to know. I knew I would never see my babies again."

Carla didn't want to ask the question that was lurking in her mind, she didn't want to hurt Eunice but she had to. "Sometimes certain cults use children for their sacrifices."

Oh, she shouldn't have said that.

Eunice began to sob softly, wiping away her tears, all she was able to squeak out before another contraction took hold was, "I know."

When the contraction ended, Carla turned the two of them around and headed back to camp. "I'm sorry all these bad things happened to you Eunice. I didn't know."

"That's why I'm telling *you*," she told her adamantly. "I feel I need to warn you. If you don't obey God, the monster will get you one way or the other."

You're nuts.

"I don't believe that," Carla answered her with a stern tone. "The God I serve is a God of love. He wouldn't allow that."

"But are you sure you're serving *Him*?

"Of course, I'm sure."

"Then act like it before it's too late. Please! Take it from me, sin isn't worth it. You need to repent and change your lifestyle before you get yourself stuck in a mess like me. I don't have any hope left, but *you* might have a chance still"

The woman was starting to scare her. Was she insane? "You have hope."

"Not anymore," Eunice said. "My *scars* finally disfigured my soul. I know what's right, but I can't change. I know that now. I've accepted my fate. No matter what I do, I know I have to go back to my sinful lifestyle. I need to protect my kids. And you know what will happen the moment I go back? Zach will suck me in like he always does. Besides, if I don't go back, not only will Zach find me and beat me, that's a given, but he will take my kids and never let me see them again. Then who will protect them?"

"I still believe you have hope."

"No, *you* have hope. It's simple for you. Just repent."

"I repent every day." Carla was getting angry now. Who did this woman think she was? She didn't know her heart. Only God knew her heart

"But you never change your lifestyle," Eunice argued, talking against another contraction. "You do the same thing over and over, even though you know it's wrong."

"I'm weak," Carla fumed, wishing the woman would shut up. "What can I say?"

"Well," Eunice winced with pain, pausing for a moment. "Your weak will is putting you at risk for a lot of evil. Your giving the devil a foothold, did you know that? You're letting evil in. It's everywhere. I can feel it here right now. It's after you. Believe me, I've learned to recognize the signs after fifteen years of disobedience."

Good for you, now shut up!

"I think you should sit around the fire with the others," Carla said trying to change the topic of conversation as they neared the camp.

"Don't change the subject."

I can if I want to. Carla knew she didn't like this woman right from the start, her niceties and sudden interest in her salvation hadn't changed a thing. Without a doubt she was not her friend. In fact, the others should know about her being in labour. This would be a perfect time to tell them.

As the two women approached the fire, Carla opened her mouth to tell them about Eunice, but before she could say a word, something rumbled beneath her feet.

The group immediately stood up, looked at each other, and wondered what was going on. But Carla didn't have to wonder, she already knew. She'd been through it many times in California, and she told them straight out.

"Earthquake!"

Chapter 12

Pip felt the explosion beneath him, it was a big one. He was glad he wasn't still down there. Nobody would have survived.

The force of the blow sent waves and bubbles to the surface, churning the men in different directions like a washing machine. Pip did all he could to keep his head above water, but Cutter was having trouble.

"Cutter!" Adam shouted, turning himself around in a circle as the big man suddenly went under. "Where are you?"

Mike paid no attention to the two men, and kept on swimming without looking back. Pip wondered if he was deaf. Adam was shouting so loudly, it could have wakened the dead.

For a moment, Pip considered doing what Mike was doing. He could pretend he didn't notice anything, head to the island, save himself and let the others drown. After all, it was his only chance to escape these men.

But no, Pip wasn't like that. Grandfather and Grayling had taught him too well. He turned himself around, fighting the current, and headed back to Adam.

"Cutter went down!" Adam shouted, coming up for air. "What do we do?"

Pip dove down head first into the swirling water to look for Cutter, but he couldn't see a thing, the water was too murky from the explosion. When he popped his head above the surface and took a breath, he couldn't believe what he saw.

The monster had risen from the depths of the earth to strike again, right there in front of him. It was as if a video game was playing in slow motion.

An enormous black eel-like creature, the one he had been tracking, rose before the men like a prehistoric dinosaur. In his mouth was a body, crushed between its sharp jagged teeth, arms and legs flailing like a captured bug.

Blood oozed and dripped from the corner of the creatures mouth as it hovered in the water, staring Pip straight in the eye. It crunched now, hard against Cutter's body, breaking it in half as it fell to the swirling waves beneath.

Pip tread water, watching in horror, unable to move. Adam swam as fast as he could, and caught up with Mike who had taken one look at the beast, swam as fast as he could, and dragged himself to safety on a rock that edged the island.

Pip remained where he was.

The beast just stared at him through his beady slit eyes, jaws half-open, blood still fresh and dripping as if to say, "Look what I can do."

Within moments, the creature retreated, and dove down into the deep where he came from. Pip flipped to his back and back-paddled toward shore, sure that they hadn't seen the last of *him*.

~~~~

"It's over," Carla informed them. "It was just a tremor. We're lucky."

Sadie didn't care if it *was* just a tremor, it was alarming enough to make her want to get out of there immediately. "I'm getting out of here! I can't stay here. *We* can't stay here," she shouted, not realizing everyone was paying attention to Eunice.

Eunice had collapsed to the ground while Carla knelt beside her and the other two men busily unwrapped her foot.

"It's not her foot," Carla kept saying.

Sadie ran to Eunice and knelt beside her, putting her arm around the woman. "It must be awfully painful dear."

Her foot had worsened in a very short time. It wasn't only green, the flesh looked like it was melting right off her. It went all the way up to her knee now."

Brian bandaged it again, covering her leg like a cast.

"I don't know what this is," Brian said, "but it's progressing so fast it makes me think it might be flesh eating disease. Nobody touches it but me. Are we clear?"

Everyone echoed him like they were robots.

Eunice murmured a long guttural moan and grunted in agony, "Just kill me now, and get it over with."

"We'll take care of your leg honey," Sadie tried to calm her. "Don't you worry."

"It's not her leg," Carla kept on saying.

Then, Eunice started to scream, constricting her body like a caterpillar after someone touched it. The two men kneeling at her foot suddenly backed away.

"My knees are all wet," Shepherd said, looking white as a ghost.

"I tried to tell you guys!" Carla said.

"Tell us what?" they all yelled in unison.

"She's having the baby...*RIGHT NOW!*"

~~~~

Brian felt sick to his stomach. He didn't know what to do –but they were all still looking at him. "Let's carry her to the shelter Shepherd," he said, trying to put on a brave face. "She'll be more comfortable with the blankets in there."

Once they did that, Eunice seemed to quiet down. It brought back terrible memories for Brian. He flashed back to Jenny's Labour and Delivery room when Patrick was born. It was like a horror show.

One minute she was laying on the bed, knees up, ready to deliver, and the next minute monitors were beeping and sending off all kinds of alarms. Jenny had gone into cardiac arrest and he was told to leave, but being the kind of man that he was, he refused.

"I need to stay with my wife," he shouted as they tried to push him out of the room. "You don't understand. I'm her husband –her coach."

The nurses shoved him so hard, before he realized it, he was already out of the room. "Please, Mr. Mackie," one of the nurses said, "Give the doctors room to work."

"I have to be in there," he shouted, raking his hands through his hair, frustrated. *She needs me!*"

Then, when the nurses thought he was under control, they went back in. He did too. He snuck in through the side door and saw them splitting Jenny's belly open like a gutted fish. They yanked Patrick out and plopped him in the nurse's arms like he wasn't even important.

He wished he hadn't seen all that blood because the light-headedness that followed caused him to hit the floor like a bomb.

It wasn't pretty.

Jenny spent the next two weeks in the hospital recovering, and baby Patrick was unharmed. It all turned out good in the end, but he didn't want any more children. That changed 18 years later when they found themselves unexpectedly pregnant with Nathan. Thankfully he was nothing like his brother and labour and delivery went smoothly even though Jenny's heart was monitored daily. He still swore he never wanted to witness another birth as long as he lived.

"Brian," he heard a voice calling, snapping him back to reality. The moaning sounds told him Eunice still hadn't delivered.

"What do we do Brian?" Sadie asked him, distraught and panicked. "I don't know how to deliver a baby. None of us do. You're the only one with any kind of emergency training."

"*I'm* not doing it," he said plain and simple. "*I can't.*"

Sadie spun around with her arms in the air. "Then who's going to deliver this baby?" she asked as she looked at Shepherd with hopeful eyes.

"Don't look at me," Shepherd shrugged. "I've been in prison for the last fifteen years. I wouldn't know a thing about *woman* stuff if my life depended on it."

Brian noticed that Carla was trying to sneak away, but he called her just before she did. "What about you Carla?" he asked her. "Do you have any experience?"

The over-tanned woman with bushy blonde hair stopped in her tracks, sighed very heavily, and hung her head as she answered him. "*Yes,*" she complained. "I have experience, *plenty of it.*"

Then Eunice moaned, holding her belly. "I want Carla to deliver my baby," she grunted, "I know *she* can do it."

Carla wrenched her hands together, dried her palms against her pink sweat suit she put on this morning, and headed for the lean-to.

Sadie went to her side and draped a blanket up for privacy.

Brian and Shepherd stood around the fire, far away so they couldn't see anything, but not far enough. They could still hear Eunice wailing and screaming, and the other two women cheering her on.

"I'm *so* glad I'm a guy!" Shepherd told him.

"Me too."

The big burly man looked pale enough to pass out, probably just like Brian did to him. "You have any kids?" he asked Shepherd, desperately trying to drown out the terrible screeching sounds.

"No…You?"

"Just two," Brian answered him. "Thank the good Lord."

"Amen to *that* brother!"

Just then everything fell silent. The two men looked back at the lean-to, wondering what was going on. Then Brian heard it –the crisp clear sound of an infant crying.

Ah…what a sound.

"And that makes it all worth it," Shepherd smiled, clinking his tin cup of water against Brian's."

"*That* it does, my friend. *That* it does."

Brian was glad it was over, but something alarmed him. He could hear the baby, but not Sadie and Carla. They didn't even come out. Usually women were ecstatic at this point, jumping around telling everyone whether it was a boy or a girl.

Then he saw Sadie slink out of the lean-to. Her demeanour was sombre, not like her at all. Brian rushed over to her immediately. "What's wrong?"

Sadie just shook her head and said nothing.

Shepherd grabbed hold of the small woman and practically squeezed her in his muscular tattooed arms. She sobbed at the embrace. "What is it?" he asked her softly.

"Something's wrong with Eunice," she sobbed, "...and the baby. Carla wouldn't let me touch either of them. She told me to tell you not to come in either."

Shepherd led Sadie to the fire, and sat down with her. Brian followed them. "Tell us what you know."

Shepherd released his arms from Sadie, and let her compose herself before she spoke. "Everything was going good," she swallowed, "right up to when the baby came out. But we didn't notice the infection had spread all the way up to her thigh.

"You mean...it spread that fast?" Brian asked, getting worried now.

"Yes," she went on. "It's so bad you guys. The whole leg looks like rotting flesh." Sadie broke down, trying to finish what she was saying. "And now the baby has it too. His poor little hand touched the infection before we even realized it was there."

"So, what's going on *now*?" Shepherd asked.

"Carla's cutting the baby's fingers off with a scissors."

Oh no she's not!

Chapter 13

Carla grabbed the scissors she cut the cord with and drew them to the baby's small fingers, tears streaming down her cheeks, as Eunice lay there hidden beneath a cluster of crumpled blankets, egging her on.

"*Just do it*!" Eunice moaned like a madwoman that made no sense at all. I don't want him to suffer because of me. Just cut the infection off.

"But why?" Carla sobbed, looking at the wrinkly red-faced baby screaming in her unworthy arms. "He might *not* get the infection."

Agonizing tears burst from Carla, wishing she didn't have to do this crazy thing.

"*Just do it Carla*! Eunice screamed again, "Before it spreads like mine."

When Carla finally regained her composure and the tears in her eyes stopped blurring her vision, she sniffled and forced the baby's tightly clenched fist open, bringing the scissors to the miniature fingertips as if she were just clipping his nails.

"*STOP!*" a voice shouted from behind the privacy blanket.

"*Put the scissors down!*" Brian scolded her, coming into the lean-to, red-faced and serious. "You are *not* cutting that baby."

Sadie rushed in behind him along with Shepherd.

Carla froze, stunned at the sudden intrusion. She dropped the scissors to the ground as Sadie took the bundled baby from her. "*I didn't want to!*" she sobbed, falling to her knees beside Eunice.

"I told her to do it," Eunice explained. "The baby touched my infection. I don't want him to die like me."

Carla watched Sadie as she cradled the unharmed baby in her arms, cooing it softly, kissing his tiny forehead, then observing his fingers. "They're fine," Sadie reassured her. "His fingers are perfect...and you wiped off the puss that he touched right away. You did everything you could. Now it's up to God."

"But what if he gets sick?" Eunice sobbed, moving her body in pain.

Brian piped up, "Eunice?" he said softly, kneeling beside her. "Do you understand what is happening to you?"

"I'm dying," she continued to sob.

"The infection from the bite has taken over your body," he said as politely as a man could in these kinds of circumstances. "I don't know why, but I definitely know it was from the bite. Your baby didn't get bitten, *you* did. So, chances are he will be just fine. Shepherd got bitten too you know. His bite doesn't show any signs of infection."

Eunice's teary red eyes widened then. "I didn't know that."

"You see honey," Sadie tried to sooth Eunice. "Your baby will be fine...and we'll watch him carefully, don't you worry about that."

Eunice moaned in pain, sobbing so much she could hardly speak. "But I won't be here to hold him. I can't leave him...*alone*," she moaned, fidgeting as her body began to tremble, blood running from the corner of her mouth now.

"Give me that medical kit," Brian spoke seriously, as Carla immediately handed it to him. "I'm giving you some morphine Eunice –it will help with the pain."

Carla watched as he prepared the needle, tapped it for a second and stuck it in the woman's arm.

They all watched as her jittery body calmed down just a little.

"We'll let you ladies have some privacy now," Brian said, standing up, taking Shepherd with him as he lifted the privacy curtain and left.

When they were gone, Sadie decided to pray for Eunice. "Lord, take this woman's pain, and take her soul into your hands."

Then Eunice held up her hand to stop her. "No!" she spoke sternly. "God has turned his back on me. I failed him too many times. That's why I'm dying."

"He can forgive you," Sadie pleaded.

"*No!*" Eunice muttered. "I denied him! There *is* no more hope for me."

Carla's eyes filled with tears.

"But there's hope for my baby," Eunice sobbed, starting to tremble again. "Sadie...I want you to take care of my baby. Don't let my husband have him."

"Why not?"

"She doesn't want that," Carla interrupted as if it were her duty to speak for the dying woman she barely knew, yet, for some reason she felt an unexplainable kinship to her that scared her.

Eunice licked her dry lips and spoke again. "Tell her later Carla," she said, turning to her, eyeing her now. "And Carla...come close to me so you can hear me."

Carla knelt at her side and put her ear to Eunice's trembling mouth. "I want you to listen to someone who knows. Change while you still can. Turn from your sinful lifestyle before Satan gets a foothold on you too. Repent before your circumstances won't let you. If you don't, you're Christianity will be as dead a I will be in a few minutes. Then, all you'll have left is a corpse. You'll call yourself a Christian, but your life won't prove it. Don't be a body without a soul."

Eunice fell silent then, coughing only to let some more blood escape from her mouth. Carla drew back, gulping hard. "Eunice?"

Sadie knelt down beside Carla, still holding the cooing baby. She put one hand on Eunice's forehead and started praying again.

"No!" Eunice laboured to breathe. "I don't *want* God, I want my baby. Let me hold him one more time, so I can say goodbye."

Carla couldn't bare this anymore, she got up, wiped her eyes, and started to leave. Then, as she turned around one last time, Eunice took her last breath and passed away.

Sadie wailed as she flopped over Eunice's dead body, still holding her baby boy in her arms. "*My God*," she cried aloud. "*Take this woman into your arms!*"

Carla turned, ignoring Sadie's desperate cries, and walked away.

~~~~

Eunice's death worried Brian even though he told the others not to. The fact was, they didn't know what kind of creature bit Eunice and what caused her infection. Shepherd on the other hand didn't seem to be exhibiting the same signs as Eunice the last time he checked anyway.

They had to bury the dead woman, it was the only way to be safe.

"So now what do we do?" Shepherd asked Brian as the two of them sat around the fire with Sadie and the baby. "It's mid-afternoon already and we have to get out of here before nightfall."

"He's right Brian," Sadie admitted, still memorized by the infant in her arms. "This little one needs to be fed, and I don't have anything to feed it. I can't keep fooling him by letting him suck on my finger. He's going to figure out that it's not his mamma sooner or later."

An eerie silence fell over them at the mention of Eunice. It wasn't the fact that she died that hit so hard, it was *how* she died that made it so sad.

"I was thinking," Brian suggested, "that I should swim to shore and get some help now. I don't know that we have any other options."

"But Brian," Sadie said in a panic, "What if that *thing* bites you."

Brian didn't want to answer that. He was willing to take the chance for the sake of the baby and the others.

Then Shepherd suggested another way. "*I* can go," he said, "I've already been bitten, and nothing happened to me. Maybe I'm immune or something. It's worth a shot. Better me than you bro."

Brian didn't like his offer. *He* was the P.I that brought them out there. He was responsible, and he didn't feel like risking anyone else's life. "We should vote," he said, hoping that would put an end to Shepherd's offer. After all, the women knew him and trusted *him* more than Shepherd, not saying he wasn't a nice guy but Brian just thought it was *his* responsibility.

First, they had to find the other two women.

~~~

The island was beautiful, more beautiful than Dinah had realized. She had read about Northern Saskatchewan and it's pristine lakes, forests, and Precambrian rock formed from volcanoes, but she never pictured it like this.

The small tremor just added charm to the fascinating island, hypnotizing her to explore the jagged rocks that jetted out from the ground everywhere, as if they had a mind of their own, and the tall trees so majestic, they made her want to stay there all day. In fact, she didn't even feel like she *was* lost.

Perhaps she shouldn't have wandered away from camp this morning, but she just couldn't help it. If the Garden of Eden had been as pretty as this place, no wonder Adam and Eve didn't want to leave.

As the sun shone overhead, Dinah realized she should probably head back to camp, Sadie would be worried by now. Lucky for her, she could see the shore from where she was standing. She hadn't been lost at all, only turned around. She could even hear their voices.

As Dinah headed for camp, she started whistling, and thinking. For all the drugs she had tried in her short life, nothing compared to the natural high of *this* place and the God who created it.

After rehab, she didn't know where to turn until someone suggested Shining Star Lodge to her. There she found the brightest star ever to touch the world –Jesus Christ. She was grateful for Sadie and all she did for her. Helping her find the Savior truly had made the whole trip worth it. She would never forget this place even if the circumstances had stranded them for the moment.

She wondered if Brian had made it to shore by now. Surely a rescue boat would be coming shortly, but then she would have to go home. Not that she wasn't ready, she was, but leaving Sadie would be hard. She had been like a mother to her, giving her a new name and all.

From the moment she arrived and Sadie had heard her story, she brought out her Bible and showed her something important. "That's *you* Butterfly," Sadie told her after reading the story in Genesis 34 about the girl who had been raped like she had.

"From now on Amanda," Sadie smiled, "I would like to call you Dinah."

At first, she thought it was a little corny, but then after a while, it seemed to stick. From then on, she started calling herself Dinah. In fact, that's how Sadie led her to the Lord. She told her that God didn't turn his back on the *Dinah's* of this world, he used the ancient Biblical story to teach women that there *is* hope for them today.

Sadie told her, "We can *all* fall victim to cruel things that may happen to us throughout our lives, and these events can even spiral out of our control, destroying our innocence so much so that we cover them, burying them as adults.

"Old wounds that have never healed are like sin that never goes away. It pollutes us, destroys us, until one day…it eventually kills us. Don't choose that lifestyle, don't choose the original *Dinah's* fate Butterfly. *She* didn't have much hope in the society she grew up in. She didn't have access to counsellors or rehabilitation clinics to help her cope, but *you* do. You have friends to help you through, but more importantly, you have a *special* friend…and his name is Jesus Christ."

And that was only part of Sadie's many lesson's she taught Dinah while she was there. How could she ever repay her?

The thought of leaving Shining Star saddened Dinah, but it excited her at the same time. The Christian group home Sadie had chosen for her had a good reputation and many programs to challenge a new believer's faith.

That was exactly what she needed –to stretch her wings and fly.

As Dinah neared the rocky beach, she saw something that puzzled her. It was a native man, just a little older than her. *He looks familiar?*

"Hey there," Dinah waved, trying to get the handsome teenager's attention.

The guy was either deaf or mute because he didn't seem to speak, he only waved his arms like a wild man, trying to tell her something.

"What are you trying to tell me?" she asked.

The native shushed her with a finger over his lips, alarming her with his behavior. Did he want her to go away?

Then, from somewhere behind her, crunching sounds caused her to spin around, feeling a blow to the side of the head as she dropped to the ground.

Lord?

Chapter 14

Sadie sat around the campfire rocking the screaming baby in her arms, but nothing would calm the child, not even her finger. He was hungry.

What on earth was she doing taking care of a baby? What was she thinking? She had never raised a child. How could Eunice ask her to keep him? He belonged with his father, and his siblings, not *her*.

The baby's face was so red now, Sadie stood up and started walking around with him, trying to sooth the distraught infant. Where was everyone?

Help me Lord, I know not what I do!

In a way, Sadie was glad she had not married and raised a family –this was hard.

Suddenly Carla snuck up on her from behind. "I thought you might need some help," she smiled, "I heard him all the way from the beach over there. Let me have him."

Sadie handed him over to the pink woman with her long-colored fingernails and watched her work her magic. Within seconds, the baby stopped it's screeching. It was the most remarkable thing she had ever seen.

"How did you do that?"

"Experience," Carla smiled up at her and then looked back down at the calm child. "I have kids of my own. It's been a while since they were this small, but you never forget…never."

As Carla stood up, swinging her hips, body moving like she was dancing, the child cooed in her arms. "See, you got to trick him. If he thinks your calm, he'll be calm. It's a technique I learned with my first."

"How many kids do you have," Sadie asked her.

"Three…but they're all grown up now. They don't smell like this anymore," Carla said inhaling, as she smelt the top of the baby's head.

What an odd woman. Sadie wondered what she was doing *that* for.

"There's nothing like the smell of a newborns head," Carla beamed. "Just ask any mother. We don't forget the smell. Someone should bottle it, they'd make a million dollars."

"Whatever you say," Sadie grinned as they both sat down by the fire.

The baby immediately started to wail. "Oh, I think someone is hungry," Carla deducted. "We'll have to try and feed him."

"And how are we going to do that?"

Carla looked around thinking. "We have surgical gloves in the medical kit, right?"

Sadie nodded her head.

"I have a small bag of powdered milk in the cooler. Let's boil a pot of water, make some formula, and pour it in the glove. It'll work. They're the good gloves, not the kind with all that latex, and they're sterilized already."

Sadie was not too sure of this idea, but she would give it a go. "And have you ever made formula before?"

"Oh, all the time, I never did the breastfeeding thing."

Somehow, that didn't surprise her. "Okay then," Sadie agreed, listening to the hungry baby continue to wail. "We better hurry up then."

~~~~

Pip struggled as he tried to pull himself free from the rope that bound him and the young girl around the base of a tall evergreen close to shore. It was Mike's way of handling things. He thought it was better to leave them behind.

"Sorry kids," Mike said, "that monster needs a sacrifice and you two are it. Maybe he'll leave us alone if he has his fill. Besides, I don't need you any more Pippi Longstocking. It's either kill you now or leave you and sweet-cheeks here for fish bait."

Pip glared him straight in the eye and didn't say a word. All Mike did was laugh, swing his gear on his shoulder, sauntering off with Adam.

The girl on the other side of the tree, tied to his arms, was still unconscious. Pip remembered her from the lodge. Her name was Dinah. How could he forget?

From the moment Mike told him he had to stay overnight at the lodge with them so they could get early starts, he had his eye on her. She was so different from the girls he had met in this area. The obvious was her fair skin and her fair hair.

He never got to speak to her, he only admired her from afar. Sometimes he wished he had enough courage to approach women, but he never did. Perhaps that's why he still didn't have a girlfriend.

Pip could hear her moving now, groaning as she regained consciousness. *Should he say something? He should say something?* He gulped hard and decided to go for it. "Are you...are you okay?"

"What's going on?" she cried in a panic, pulling hard against the rope that bound them both to the tree trunk.

Pip didn't know how to explain. He didn't know where to begin. "We...um, we're tied up," he said, feeling like a fool for stating the obvious.

"I know *that*, but why?"

Pip took a breath. *Get over it dummy. Speak to the girl.* "I...um, I was doing some guiding for these guys, the guys who hit you over the head and tied us up. They double crossed me." He considered telling her about the monster, but didn't want to scare her.

"Was that Mike?"

"Well...yes."

"We came out here to look for him when our boat went down."

"Your boat went down?" Pip asked her without even stuttering.

"Yes, and I'm stranded here with the others. I have to warn them about Mike," she insisted tugging at the rope again. "Help me get out of this."

Pip tugged and twisted with her, trying to free at least one hand, but nothing worked, she couldn't even slip her tiny wrists out.

Then, from behind a rock, Pip heard a familiar sound.

"What was that?" Dinah asked in a panic.

A hissing sound grew louder until...they both saw exactly what it was. "Stay perfectly still," Pip ordered her, whispering softly.

The monster slithered toward the tree, slinking down low as it eyed the two of them wrapped around the stump. It's eyes were yellow with small black slanted pupils like a cat. It hissed again.

Dinah fidgeted.

The creature suddenly lunged forward, opening its jaw, ready to strike.

~~~~

Once they pierced a hole through the fingertip of the surgical glove with a sterile needle, the baby started sucking immediately. It was a wonderful sight to see. Carla watched the baby chug down his nourishment. "See, I told you it would work."

As they both sat around the fire watching the baby suck, Sadie smiled and said, "You know, isn't it so amazing how God created us? As infants, we're dependant on our mother completely, but as Adults, we think we don't need anybody but ourselves. We think we can get along in this world just fine, but we really can't. We can't do anything without God. Just like this baby, he depends on us to survive, and we depend on God."

If the woman was trying to get her to open up about the same old topic, she had another thing coming. This was neither the time nor the place to debate God.

"What do you think Carla?

Fight it Carla! Don't say a word.

"Did you hear me?"

Oh, for goodness sake, she had to say something. "Yes, I heard you," Carla snapped, "but I don't know if I agree with you."

Sadie's eyes grew wide. "What do you mean? Don't you think we're dependant on God?"

You might be, but I'm not. "We'll, it's not that simple, is it?" she said, stopping for a moment to burp the baby, patting his back ever so softly as she draped the tiny thing over her shoulder.

"Sure, it is…if you're a believer!"

Oh, here it goes –judging time. "I *am* a believer," Carla said, "I told you that before, but just because I don't think the same way as you do doesn't mean I'm a heathen. Good grief, I'm sick of people judging me."

"I'm not trying to judge you dear," Sadie sighed, looking nervous now. "I just want to know how you think, that's all."

We'll, if she really wanted to know..." Okay," Carla said, lifting the baby from her shoulders, tightening his blanket giving him the milk again. "I'll tell you how I think. I think that we *don't* have to go around talking about God every minute of the day. I think that *we* are in control of what happens to us. We can't blame God for everything."

"I see."

What did that mean? "See, now you sound like you're judging me."

"I'm sorry."

The baby started fussing so Carla tried to burp him again. "If you *people* would just listen instead of judging all the time, you might actually learn something. I think God gave us enough brains to take care of ourselves and make our own choices."

"So do I, but sometimes our choices are wrong."

Another slap in the face. "Are you insinuating that I have made wrong choices?"

"Have you?"

This conversation was starting to annoy Carla. Did she even have to answer that? "I haven't made any wrong choices."

"What about Mike?"

How dare she, how dare she even start into this topic, the same topic Eunice was stuck on, the same Bible study topic all over again. "I love Mike, and I'm sick to death that he might be injured somewhere or...dead. How can you even say what your saying?"

"I have a duty to question you."

Carla wrapped the baby and swaddled him tightly with his blanket, rocking him now. "And what duty might that be?"

"It says so in the Bible," Sadie went on, "Galatians 6:1 says, 'If a man is overtaken in any trespass, you who are spiritual, restore such a one in a spirit of gentleness.'"

"I'm not a man and I'm *not* trespassing."

"*Man* is plural for all mankind, and yes you *are* trespassing. If you claim to be a Christian, and you deliberately choose to live a sinful lifestyle with Mike, it is my responsibility as it is any fellow believer, to restore you back to spiritual health. I'm not doing it to hurt you or judge you, I'm doing it because I care about your relationship with Christ."

"Fine then," Carla fumed, "What if I say I'm *not* a believer then. Will you leave me alone?"

"*Are* you a believer?"

The whole discussion felt like Question Period to Carla. It was time to put an end to it. "That depends on the definition," she argued, hoping that would stop her.

"Let me be frank," Sadie continued anyway, clearing her throat as if she were ready to speak a sermon. "Life is short —we saw that with poor Eunice, so I'll just spit it out. Being a believer means to recognize you're a sinner and repent of your sins. It means that you believe that Jesus died on the cross for you, went to hell for you, for *your* sins so you wouldn't have to, and rose again to give you new life. Being a believer means you have a *new* life and you want to shed your old ways so you can start living your *new* life. It means you love God so much, you'll do anything to prove your love for him, and thank him for taking your punishment so you wouldn't have to suffer an eternity in hell. *That's what a believer is."*

Sadie stopped and had to catch her breath. Carla thought she was going to pass out for a minute her face was so red.

"I know all that, but some of that stuff is a little too narrow minded for me," Carla admitted. "Life is complicated. Sometimes sin just happens and it's not the end of the world. God understands."

"There is *no* exception to sin. If you know it's wrong, *don't do it.*"

Carla could tell she was getting nowhere with this woman. She meant well, but it wasn't something she hadn't heard before. She just didn't agree, that's all. Thank heaven she heard voices coming from the trees behind them.

"That would be the men," Carla interrupted Sadie just before she was about to say something else. She carefully handed Sadie the sleeping baby and stood up. "I'm going to see if they found Dinah."

As soon as Carla turned around, she caught a glimpse of Shepherd, and Brian and some others coming out of the bush. "MIKE!" she shouted, running over to greet him walking with the familiar group of faces. "I THOUGHT YOU WERE DEAD!"

"Me dead?" Mike smiled as Carla jumped-hugged him so hard he almost fell over. "You know me better than that babe. I would *never* die and leave you all alone. Not in a million years."

They kissed long and hard, and Carla didn't care *who* was judging her now. Her boyfriend was alive and well, and it had *nothing* to do with God. "They sunk my boat baby. Do *you* have a way out of here?"

"We're kind of stuck too, but don't you worry about anything babe," Mike smiled as he held up something in his hand. "I have a radio and I already called for help."

Chapter 15

The creature was toying with them.

The gigantic snake, eel, or whatever it was that seemed to be holding Dinah and Pip captive, just lay there observing the two of the them bound to the tree as if he were waiting for the right moment to devour them.

It would get up, using its pigmy webbed feet and slink around them every now and then, but it wouldn't go away.

Dinah had never seen anything like it before. The creature was massive, and shiny black like a sea lion. She wondered if it was a pre-historic fish.

"How long do you think it will stay here?" Dinah whispered.

"I don't know."

"Can I ask you something?" she went on.

"Shoot."

"Do you think the creature thinks we were left here for him?"

Dinah heard nothing from the other side but a small shush. When she turned her head, she knew why. The creature was right at her ear.

His large open mouth trembled beside her, almost touching her cheek. She could feel his warm breath against her skin, sending a chill up her spin. His half-pursed mouth revealed his white jagged teeth and a long red snake-like tongue.

Saliva from the creature's mouth dripped in her lap as he hovered in front of her almost as if he were reading her mind. *Jesus, help me!*

Then the creature started to hiss at her, mutating into a low earthy growl.

The Lord is my shepherd...I will fear no evil.

Then, as if startled by something, the creature retreated, slithering into the bush.

Breathe!

"Dinah?" she heard Pip ask her, still whispering. "Did it hurt you?"

At first, nothing would come out of her mouth. Her lips wouldn't move though her brain tried to speak. Then with a little effort, the words started forming. "I…I'm okay…How about you?"

"I'm fine, but I'll be even better when we get out of here. I have a feeling it's going to come back for us, and when it does…it'll be hungry."

The two of them pulled against the rope again, struggling with each other to free themselves, giving up from exhaustion after only a few minutes. "It's hopeless," Dinah cried, "we'll never get out of here."

"Don't panic," Pip tried to calm her down. "Let's just think. Do you have a pocket-knife on you, or anything sharp?"

Dinah thought for a minute, what did she do with Carla's nail file? She was so sick of the arrogant woman pampering her nails while they were on the boat that she took the file when she wasn't looking. Did she shove it in her jean pocket before she put her wetsuit on, or did she leave it somewhere else?

"Pip?" she said, "I'm not sure, but I think I have a nail file in my back pocket. See if you can reach it with me."

Dinah's petite arm almost wrenched out of its socket as the two of them forced their arms to work together to check her back pocket. *Walla,* she was right.

"There it is," Pip said, fingering the tool in his hand. "You're amazing Dinah!"

She couldn't remember the last time a guy told her that and actually meant it without expecting something in return. "Thanks!" she told him. "You're not so bad yourself."

Why did I say that? Dinah felt her face heat up, wishing she hadn't said the corny comeback. Thankfully, he couldn't see her blushing.

~~~

Night had already fallen on the island leaving moonlit shadows everywhere, while a distant Loon echoed beyond the horizon. A bonfire roared as Sadie sat on a rock cradling the sleeping newborn, Carla and Mike snuggled by the fire, and Brian prepared himself to go with Shepherd.

"Find her Brian," Sadie told them both before they took off into the night. "Something is wrong. I know it. Dinah wouldn't just wander off and not come back. She's a responsible girl."

"We'll find her Sadie," Brain replied. "I promise. We won't leave without her. How long did you say it would be before your friend gets here Mike?"

Mike turned from the woman he was smooching with, frowned as the flickering flame revealed annoyance in his face, and snapped out an irritated reply. "*I don't know.* He'll get here when he gets here, now buzz off and leave us alone?"

And this from the man whom they were trusting to get them off the island.

Mike turned back to what he was doing, ignoring everyone else. Sadie looked at Shepherd, and Shepherd looked at Brian, all of them saying the same thing with their eyes *–Don't trust Mike.*

"We won't be gone long Sadie," Shepherd told her just to reassure her that she wouldn't be alone with these strangers the entire night. "And we'll find Dinah too."

Shepherd put a hand on Brian's shoulder as they set out through the dark trees with nothing but a small flashlight. "I have a bad vibe about those two guys Brian."

"So do I, but let's keep quiet until we're far enough away."

The two of them walked in silence, listening to the crunching sounds beneath their feet, and the distant giggles that radiated from the flickering campfire.

Shepherd had a funny feeling he had seen Mike somewhere before, and since he hadn't been anywhere but prison for fifteen years, that narrowed the search quite a bit.

"Can we talk now," Shepherd asked Brian.

Brian stopped for a minute and looked around. "We should be far enough away."

"Good, because I don't trust Mike. I think I saw him in the Pen. If he's the same guy, he did six months for fraud and the guy he hung around with is pretty ruthless."

"Are you sure?"

"Positive."

Brian appeared as agitated as Shepherd felt. "Look," Brian whispered, "I don't feel right about leaving Sadie and the baby with them. I don't know what Mike's up to, but his story about help coming seems a little fishy. Something's not right. Those two guys are so shady I'd bet my life on it, and I'm usually a pretty good judge of character."

"Me too. I get the same vibe, but what exactly did you have in mind?"

"Well, I don't buy their story about Dinah. They said they saw her take off in a boat with some guy.

Sadie said she would *never* do that, not even if she thought she would be able to get help for us. If she had access to a boat, she would have come for us by now, don't you think?"

"Exactly. So, you think they made the whole story up?"

"Not only that, but their hiding something. Let's just look at this from another perspective," Brian continued as they stood there talking. "Dinah took off this morning and she hasn't been seen since. What does that usually mean?"

"Definitely *not* something good."

"Right. So, assuming they ran into her like they say they did, and assuming you're right about who Mike is –What do you *think* happened?"

"Oh man, I don't even want to go there"

Brian shook his head, "I don't either, but we have to look at every angle. She might be out there wandering around somewhere, she might be on a boat with some guy, or…she *might* be dead."

"Seriously, you think she's dead?"

"I don't know, but I intend to find out –and not by wandering around the island all night on a wild goose chase, but by going back to where we know we can get some answers. If we want to find Dinah, our best bet is to start with the last person who *claims* they saw her, and that's Mike."

"But what about Sadie?" Shepherd asked. "What do we tell *her*?"

Brian stood there mute for a minute, scratching his head. "We can't tell her we think something bad happened to her, definitely not, and I don't want to lie. Let's give this search an honest effort for about and hour. We won't go far. We'll come back and tell Sadie we couldn't find her –then we'll give Mike a little talking too –in private."

"But what if we *do* find her Brian?"

"Great! But I have a hunch that we won't. Trust me, I've dealt with situations like this before and their usually not pretty. I could be wrong, but chances are *they* know *exactly* where she is."

After wandering around the bush for an hour, Shepherd and Brian neared the camp again, seeing the bonfire through the trees. "So, we tell them we couldn't find her?" Shepherd asked, just to be sure of the plan.

"Right."

But when they got back to camp, nobody was there.

Chapter 16

Mike's friend had finally come to rescue them. Too bad Shepherd and Brian had just taken off to find Dinah, or they could have fit everyone in the large beaten old Tugboat without having to make a second trip.

Carla was more than happy to see her boyfriend again, but something seemed different about him, especially when his friend told him to hurry before the others got back. *Why wouldn't he tell him to wait?*

The Mike she knew would have been a lot more caring than that.

"But we can't leave without Dinah and the others?" Sadie pleaded with the group as she boarded the Tugboat with the sleeping baby bundled in her arms.

"*Shut her up!*" Mike's friend ordered, "Or I'll have to shut her up."

Carla didn't know what was going on here but something was wrong. Usually Mike didn't let anyone talk to him that way. "*Baby?*" she whispered, sitting next to Mike as the boat started slowly pulling away from shore. "What's going on?"

"Shut your pie hole!" Mike snapped back annoyed at her, adding several swear words to his insult, bringing tears to Carla's wondering eyes as she turned away from him and stared straight into Sadie's wide eyes.

Sadie just silently grabbed her trembling hand and squeezed.

What would make him act this way? It certainly wasn't like him to cut her down in public, though he'd done it in private several time. Usually, he was always so worried about his image to cause a scene. In fact, most of the time he put on a real show of affection whenever the two of them were in the public eye. He had to look good you know –that was just the way Mike was.

Something must have upset him. His big friend didn't exactly look like the rescuing type when he arrived with the Tugboat. He didn't even get off the boat when he arrived. Mike had to come to him.

Now as they slowly skirted the island, Carla wondered why she had even fallen for a guy like Mike. Sure, he was young and good-looking, but she was sick of the way he treated her –and now, in front of everyone. She felt like a puppy that had just been scolded.

Well she was no puppy.

Why did she always have to feel like the underdog in this relationship? Even though she was the one with all the money, he still had control as if it were all his. Well nothing was his. She paid for the entire trip, the boat, the supplies…everything, and as soon as they get back to the lodge, she'll let him have a piece of her mind.

As Carla watched Sadie cradle the sleeping infant in her arms, she couldn't help but remember her own children at that age. It seemed like a lifetime ago when she and John first started out. Things were different then –*he* was different then.

If it hadn't been for that stupid church they were attending at the time, she and John might still have a good marriage. But no, they had to start poking at their lifestyle. It wasn't her fault she had money. They were probably just jealous.

"You should give some of your inheritance to the tithe," one of the elders told her and John as they stood in the foyer of the church, Carla cradling her firstborn in her arms.

She remembered the rage that tore through her at the time. It was so hard to bite her tongue, and in different circumstances she probably would have, but not this time, this time she had just delivered a baby and her hormones were all over the place.

"I don't see that it's any of *your* business," Carla spit out, feeling the heat radiate from her cheeks. "I can do whatever I want with my money."

"But the church needs a new nursery Mrs. Reece," the elder informed her. "How do you think we're going to pay for *that*? You'll be using it too. Aren't you the least bit concerned about the financial responsibilities of the church, or are you just one of those people that think churches survive on thin air?"

"How dare you," Carla snapped. "My father worked hard for this money. I'm not about to just give it away, no matter how much you and your church try to bully me."

John fidgeted beside her. "I think what my wife is trying to say here, is that we hadn't thought about what to do with the money just yet."

"*No John*," Carla fumed, turning red like a beet. "I'm not giving any of my father's money to this church."

John looked very uncomfortable, and tried to change the subject.

"So, you don't care about God then," the elder argued.

"What does that have to do with anything?"

The elder smiled like a Cheshire cat. "It has plenty to do with it. If you're not willing to give a tenth of your money to help the church, you might as well kiss heaven goodbye. I can find the scripture to support that little fact too if you don't mind waiting."

"Oh, stick it up your…"

"*Carla*!" John stopped her before she could finish her sentence. "*That's enough!*"

The last thing Carla could remember, the baby started crying, and she stormed out of the church, thinking she'd never step foot in *that* church again.

But she did…the very next Sunday.

John calmed her down and convinced her to give her tithe. "Be a good Christian," he told her. "You'll be blessed with an abundance of love in return."

Well she received everything *but* love. The 1000 sq ft nursery was built three months later, and she sat in there only once. Once was all it took for her to know what the other women thought of her. They shunned her, talked behind her back and gossiped about everything under the sun.

For three years she endured this torture, and every time the church needed something, they always came to *her*. "Be a good Christian," her husband's voice came to mind each time. And so, she did…but no *love* ever came of it.

Then, she gave birth to her second child and it started all over again. The church needed to expand. So many new kids. They needed Sunday school rooms, a Children's Church activity center, and a gymnasium for the youth. "Your kids are going to benefit from all of this Carla," the same elder told her.

Unfortunately, her kids did not. It was the last straw. "I can't do it anymore," she told her husband. "I don't want to serve a God that rewards greed, and I don't want to belong to a church that doesn't love. I'm done."

Well almost immediately, they left the church, never to return to it again. It was almost five years before they started going to another one. Now as Carla looked back, it was way too long. Bitterness grew, and the faith of her childhood withered away.

"You can pray," a soft voice interrupted her thoughts, bringing her mind back to the cold dark night in the Tugboat, rumbling over the choppy water.

"What did you say?" Carla asked Sadie, figuring she was the one that was talking.

"I said you can pray," Sadie whispered next to her. "That's what *I* do when I'm scared. I pray...and God always sees me through. He can do that for you too you know."

Carla knew, but she didn't think it would do her any good. She hadn't prayed for a long time. She didn't even remember how. "We'll be fine," she said, faking her confidence just to put the woman at ease.

"How about if *I* pray for us," Sadie went on, trying to keep her voice down so the men wouldn't hear.

Carla gazed over at Mike, in full conversation with the other two guys, and decided it was okay. "Just a short one then," she whispered. "But it has to be quiet."

As the Tugboat chugged, Carla noticed they were going round and round the island for some reason. Perhaps Mike cared about the others after all. They were probably looking for them with that big spotlight they beamed toward the shore.

Maybe she didn't need to pray after all? Maybe Mike was just upset because he didn't want to make a second trip. Carla's head bobbed around, wondering what they were doing. *I don't need to pray. This will all work out.*

She remembered something from her Bible, "This too shall pass." And it *was* passing. Mike was already smiling. His demeanour was changing to his old self again. But before Carla could tell Sadie she didn't need to pray; the woman was already mumbling her prayer.

"Keep us safe dear Lord," Sadie whispered, one arm cradling the sleeping baby and the other hand holding Carla's hand. "Take care of Dinah, and Brian, and Shepherd, and this wee one in my arms…"

Carla tried to pay attention. She tried to keep her head bowed, but something was going on. The men were excited, Mike was almost giggling. *That's my Mike. He's back.*

Suddenly the boat slowed to a crawl. Sadie stopped praying mid-sentence, and Carla stood up, pulling her hand from Sadie's. "What is it Mike?" she asked, but he didn't respond.

The men were shouting now, excited by something they saw on shore.

"It's Brian!" Sadie cried, smiling as she stood up. Carla felt the adrenaline rush as she watched the men rushing about the boat reaching for something.

"Over here!" she heard voices on shore, figures visible with the spotlight, waving their arms in the air like castaways about to be rescued.

But then, without warning…Sadie's excitement, and Carla's adrenaline rush turned to a shocking horror as shots rang out from within the boat.

~~~~

"*They're shooting at us!*" Brian shouted, ducking for cover behind a rock, hoping Shepherd had enough sense to take cover as well. "Shepherd?...Talk to me man."

"I'm over here," he yelled from behind a rock, breathing hard enough for Brian to hear him, but not see him. "I'm hit."

"How bad?"

"They got my shoulder."

Brian sighed, "Great...Just stay put. I'll try to get to you."

As the shooting peppered the jagged boulders that surrounded them, Brian jumped into the shadows darting behind the rocks until he reached Shepherd. The faint light revealed a small wound on the top of his shoulder. "You are lucky man...it just grazed you."

"No kidding."

As soon as the shooting stopped, Brian popped his head up and saw an old Tugboat pull to shore. "They're coming after us. Let's move."

Shepherd and Brian crouched as they ran to another larger group of rocks. Brian wondered why they were shooting at them in the first place. If this was their rescue boat, his assumptions were right about Mike and his buddy.

That meant Sadie and the baby were also in trouble and there was no way he would leave her with them. "Listen up Shepherd," Brian panted as they both caught their breath against a cold rock. "We're not running anymore; do you hear me. They think that's what we're going to do, but we're not. We're going toward them. They won't expect us to do that. Then we'll take the boat."

"Take the boat?" Shepherd whispered. "And just how are we going to do that?"

"You go one way, and I'll go another. We'll try to stay under the radar and we'll meet up at the boat."

"I don't know about that pal," Shepherd said with an uneasy tone. "Maybe we ought to wait it out."

"Wait it out?" Brian said. "We can't wait it out. Sadie might be on that boat."

"But she might *not* be."

"I'm not willing to take that chance Shepherd. She's a friend of mine and I'm responsible…She's got the baby too. Besides, these guys are bad news. Who knows what they're capable of…or what they're even after?

"I think *I* know."

"You do?"

"Yah," Shepherd sighed, "I think they're after *me*."

~~~~

If Ice thought this was a game, then game on, Shepherd decided. There was no way he was going to let that imbecile harm these good people. He could never live with himself if that happened, especially because *he* was the one they wanted.

Sure, he had made a mistake by not telling Brian the truth about how he arrived on the island, but now was his chance to redeem himself. *Thank you, Lord.*

"Spit it out Shepherd," Brian insisted, "What do you mean they're after you?"

"Okay, you know how I told you I just got out of prison? Well, that part is true, but I *wasn't* fishing. My boat didn't sink. I…um…sort of fell out of a bush plane. Me and this guy named Ice were fighting. He don't like me too much."

"Go on."

Shepherd could tell Brian was annoyed and disappointed with him. He didn't mean to lie, he was just embarrassed by the whole situation. How could he explain falling out of a plane? It sounded ridiculous not to mention crazy. Nobody would have believed him. But, the lesson in all this was obviously something God wanted to teach him – There is definitely *no* exceptions when it comes to sin, no matter how hard it is to tell the truth.

He told Brian the quick version of the story and then looked up over the boulder, making sure they hadn't been spotted. "So, what do you think?" he asked Brian, hoping he still had a friend.

"I think you *should* have been honest with me from the beginning."

"Oh, come on," Shepherd complained, "don't be ticked. I did the best I could. Give a con a break man. I'm not perfect."

"Fine," Brian mumbled, finishing his statement with a whisper. "You're forgiven, as long as that's everything. You're not hiding anything else, are you?"

"No."

"Good, then let's move before they come this way. You take the left. I'll take the right."

Chapter 17

The baby started screaming.

Sadie just paced the wood floor of the old Tugboat and jiggled the flailing infant, trying to calm him down. Her heart beat so loudly in her chest that she thought she was about to have a heart attack.

Jesus, help me!

Carla bawled as she sat and watched Mike and Adam darting around the different rock formations on the shore of the island looking for Brian and Shepherd.

If it wasn't for the guy they called, Ice, holding a gun on them, Sadie would have taken the baby and Carla off the boat and ran for cover like Brian and Shepherd were doing. But that was impossible now.

"Shut the kid up!" Ice yelled for the third time, pointing the gun at her.

"I'm trying!" Sadie told him, raising her voice above the screeching infant.

"Leave her alone," Carla shouted, "She's not hurting anyone. Why don't you just let us go if we're such a *bother*?"

Ice sauntered around them like a prison guard, playing with his gun. "Because," he said, "as soon as we're done playing around *here*, we're going to have some fun back at the lodge…if you know what I mean."

"You've *got* to be kidding," Carla fumed. "If that's all you want, you can have it right now you pervert. Here…take whatever you want, but let Sadie and the baby go."

Carla lifted her shirt and started pulling it over her head when Sadie grabbed her sleeve and yanked her backward to talk to her. "Don't," Sadie pleaded, shaking her head while she rocked the baby.

"Let me go!" Carla bawled in anger. "I don't *care* anymore. You think it matters? I've slept with so many guys —one more creep doesn't make a difference."

Ice wrenched his head backward and laughed so hard it startled both women. "You're pathetic," he snickered, "Mike was right about you."

"What did you say?"

"Calm down Carla," Sadie cried, pulling Carla aside so Ice couldn't hear them talk. She helped Carla put her top back on and jiggled the baby again. He was still fussy but not as loud as before so she could at least hear herself think. "Sit down and listen to me for a minute, will you?"

Carla sniffled and sat down with Sadie. "What?" she whispered, cross-armed and defensive.

Sadie looked around, making sure Ice wasn't listening. He had regained his usual position blocking the exit, standing there like a hit man. "You can't get so upset," she said, "Our lives depend on it. Please, calm down!"

"Did you here what he said to me?"

"He's just trying to get you upset."

"We'll I *am* upset," Carla raised her voice a little more than Sadie wanted. She brushed the flowing tears from her cheeks. "Wake up and smell the roses. This is my *life*, preacher woman, and it ain't so cut and dry like you seem to think life should be. Mike is my boyfriend. I *love* him...or at least I thought I did. I trusted him and now look what he's doing. I gave everything to him, and he obviously played me like a fool. Do you know what that's like? Do you? Of course not. What would a middle-aged self-righteous holier than thou *bush woman* know about the *real* world?"

Bush woman?

Sadie kept her eye on Ice. As long as he was pre-occupied, she could continue to talk. "You might think I'm naïve Carla," she said, "but I'm not. I can see you're in pain. You gave your heart to a man that abused it. I get that. But listen to me, *he* may have rejected you but *God* never has. Why don't you invest you heart in *Him* before it's too late? What if we die here tonight?"

Carla didn't answer, she just sat there thinking. Sadie looked at the baby, sleeping now like a little angel. Brian and Shepherd were out there amongst the rocky shore somewhere...and Dinah...She mumbled a prayer under her breath for *all* of them.

Nothing seemed to be happening on shore right now. The spot light was still on as well as the ship light so they could see each other, but she couldn't hear any gunfire.

Ice still stood there with his gun.

"Do you really think we might die out here tonight?" Carla suddenly continued the conversation with a whisper.

"I don't know," Sadie said, "I hope not. But if they get Brian and Shepherd, we're in trouble for sure."

"So, you think I should make things right with God?"

"Well that depends...Do you want to?"

"I don't know," Carla sighed. "My mother says I asked Jesus into my heart when I was four like I told you before, but I don't remember. I'm sure I must have because I spent so much of my childhood at church, I could recite the entire Bible by memory."

"That doesn't make you a believer."

"I *am* a believer," Carla snapped back so loudly it made Ice give them a long cold stare. "Sorry, I guess I should whisper."

Sadie wrapped the sleeping baby more tightly and focused on Carla again.

"Something my mother always said was that no matter what, I couldn't lose my salvation. Once I became a believer, I was one for life. Don't you think that's true?"

Sadie prayed for wisdom. She didn't even know how to answer the woman. Of course, she believed that you couldn't lose your salvation, yet...How could a person just go and live any way they please and still call themselves a believer?

"I think," Sadie continued very slow and cautiously, "that God sees your heart. What's in *your* heart Carla? Does Jesus Christ mean so much to you that you would do anything for him...even if it meant you had to die?"

Carla pondered on that thought for a minute. "Actually, I never thought of it quite like that before," she said. "I guess I never really think about Jesus. I know a lot about him, but if I were to die for him, I'd really have to love him, wouldn't I?"

"Like you love Mike."

"Don't even go there right now Sadie."

"Well...you know what I mean," Sadie said, feeling the boat tip just a little.

"I know what you mean, and when you put it that way, I guess Christianity doesn't mean a whole lot to me. But I know it should. I mean, I understand it, but I never have been able to move pass the understanding and change the way I live."

"Bingo!" Sadie smiled, "You just hit the nail on the head. Congratulations, you found the missing link. You need to make a decision Carla. The flesh and the spirit are in a constant battle and you need to choose one or the other…tonight!"

Sadie stood in her excitement just as the boat started to sway. Carla grabbed a hold of her and set her back down, watching the drama unfold.

Ice lost his balance with the swaying, dropping the gun somewhere on deck. The boat teetered back and forth as a figure hopped over the side and stood before him. With one swift boot to the lower jaw, Ice crumpled to the floor in pain.

Brian stood before him, dirty and wet.

"Well, well, well," he chided, "Who do we have here? If it isn't Mr. Leon Eaglefeather himself. How long has it been …five years?"

~~~~

As Brian held Leon in a chokehold kneeling down beside him on the ships deck, he couldn't believe this character was involved in all this. The last time he saw him was during the Shooting Star incident. He and his buddies had been up to no good then too.

A sudden pain hit his stomach as he recalled the sickening memories. Leon had brutally slaughtered innocent people almost killing him in the process. It was a nightmare five years ago that he thought he'd never wake up from…and now the man was back.

"I thought you went to prison for life," Brian spit, still holding Leon in a chokehold wrestling him on the ground.

The tall Indian suddenly went limp like a rag-doll, answering Brian in a cold monotone voice. "You cannot hold an eagle in bondage my friend, for he shall sore with wings that stretch far beyond the human eye."

You're not my friend and you don't scare me.

Brian knew Leon was trying to intimidate him with his native legend talk but he wasn't going to give him any more opportunity to play with his mind. "Sadie," he called to her, "hand me that rag...and the rope in the corner. I just caught me an eagle."

As Brian bound and gagged Mr. Eaglefeather and set him in the corner of the Tugboat, Shepherd crawled on board dripping wet. "Turn off the lights so they can't find us," he shouted out of breath.

"I knew you could make it buddy," Brian patted Shepherd on the back.

"I almost *didn't*," Shepherd sighed, bending over with his hands on his knees, looking as though he was about to pass out.

Brian put the boat in reverse and slowly backed the craft up so they could get out of there. "Go take a look at what I gagged and bagged," he told Shepherd.

With one glace at their captive, Shepherd collapsed to the floor.

"I got him," Carla said rushing to the rescue helping Shepherd back to his feet and guiding him to a seat. "You must be out of shape there Tinkerbelle."

"I know him!" Shepherd cried. "He's the guy."

"What guy?"

"His name is Ice." Sadie informed them.

"Yah, that's right," Shepherd said, looking like he had seen a ghost. "I know him from prison Brian. He's the *guy*."

Oh, that guy.

Obviously, Shepherd didn't want to reveal his little secret to the women about how he *really* arrived on the island, so Brian decided he'd keep his mouth shut too. Leon Eaglefeather or "Ice" as they called him was dangerous regardless of the name.

The whole thing just made Brian shake his head. If Leon was capable of breaking out of a maximum-security prison, commandeering a bush plane using Shepherd as his expendable puppet, arriving in a Tugboat…He must be up to something big.

And what exactly did Mike and Adam have to do with it?

So many questions and no answers. It wasn't exactly what you would call a good scenario, but it did make for good detective work. Brian hadn't counted on this when he decided to take on Carla Reece's job offer.

It was puzzling he had to admit, but innocent people were involved just like last time at Shooting Star and that made his skin crawl. Nobody was going to die under his care *this* time as long as he could help it. *Lord…I think I need you.*

As the old Tugboat crawled away something caught Brian's eye. It was as if someone lit a match near a jagged cliff as the boat passed beneath it.

Suddenly something hit the wood floor of the Tugboat. Glass exploded into flames when Brian realized it was a Molotov cocktail. *"Get some buckets!"* he shouted. Sadie screamed, holding the baby tightly to her chest. Carla fluttered about looking for a bucket, and Shepherd tried to put the fire out with the wet shirt he ripped off his back…But nothing would stop the flames from engulfing the boat.

Chapter 18

One last flame flickered in the water as the final tip of the Tugboat went under. Carla, Brian, and Shepherd tread water beside it. "Where's Sadie...and the baby?" Carla shouted in a panic, spinning her wet hair around looking for the woman.

The three of them swam in circles calling out her name until they heard a faint cry of a baby in the distance.

"There she is," Shepherd pointed.

All Carla could see was a small figure bobbing up and down in the water about five hundred feet in front of them. She tried to swim as fast as the two men, but she just couldn't keep up. "Is the baby all right?" she shouted anyway, knowing Brian and Shepherd would find out before she could.

Nobody answered her back.

Carla continued to swim until she caught up with everyone. Then she saw the poor thing floating in Sadie's arms as the two men tried to hold her head above water.

The baby was cold and lethargic and wasn't crying now at all. Carla knew if they didn't get him warm soon, he wasn't going to make it.

"We need to get to shore," Brian insisted. "So, follow me. We drifted pretty far out, so it's important we stay together as a group."

"But I'm so c-cold," Sadie whispered in a shaky voice. "And the b-baby isn't even m-moving anymore."

"He'll be okay Sadie," Brian said, "Just keep kicking your legs.

But Carla knew it wasn't okay. These northern waters were still pretty cold even if it *was* August.

She was even shivering uncontrollably. She couldn't imagine a newborn infant surviving this.

"Where do you think Ice is?" Shepherd asked as he dogpaddled with the group.

"With his arms and legs tied up, he shouldn't be bothering us ever again," Brian said. "Now all we have to worry about is Mike and Adam."

Carla cringed when he said Mike. She couldn't help but feel responsible for the damage he caused. "You leave Mike up to me," she said, "It's my fault we're drowning like rats right now so the least I could do is talk to him for you."

"No... Carla!" Brian snapped back, "He's dangerous. I don't want you doing anything. I'll handle him...Do you hear me?"

"He's *not* dangerous, *really*. I know him, and he wouldn't have done any of this unless he was coaxed into it somehow."

"It doesn't matter," Brian fumed. "You leave him up to me. All I want you to do when we get to shore is start a fire and get that baby warm. Got it?"

"*I got it.*" But she didn't want to. Mike was her responsibility. Not only that, she needed to talk to him first before anyone else. She needed to know what was going on.

As the group continued to swim toward shore in the cold dark water, Carla felt something bump her leg as she kicked. It didn't feel like a rock or someone else's foot. It felt like someone was actually tickling her foot.

She thrashed her legs about.

Then, with great force, something pulled her underwater. "*Help!*" she shouted in a panic, feeling something pulling her leg.

Her arms did nothing for her –even her legs were useless. Something had a hold of her and wouldn't let her go.

Water went up her nose, and burned her throat as she screamed underwater. Bubbles formed as she fought with all her might. But whatever had her leg, had a good hold on it, and pulled her deeper and deeper away from the others.

I can't see.

If it wasn't nighttime the water wouldn't be so dark, but it was and she had no control in this frightful situation. Then…just before her lungs filled completely with water, a set of glowing yellow eyes appeared before her face.

~~~~

"What's happening?" Sadie cried, hoping Shepherd would give her some answers. Carla went under and Brian dove down to get her, but where are they?

"I don't know Shepherd answered her back, lets just keep moving."

Everything was falling apart. Sadie couldn't believe it. Her body shook from hypothermia as she forced herself to keep on kicking. She supported the newborns bobbing head in one hand as she swam with the other.

"It's too late for the baby," she sobbed in a raspy voice. The small infant was naked and stone cold. His blanket had floated away the moment they hit the water. His tiny body was lifeless and stiff, doing the dead man's float with arms out to the sides and pigmy legs sprawled apart.

"Just keep moving Sadie."

"I c-can't," she continued to sob, "I-look at *him*."

Overhead, the rumbling sounds of thunder echoed the night skies. Lightning flashed in the distance, lighting their sombre faces as they observed the lifeless child, prostrate to the heavens.

"I promised Eunice I'd take care of him," she bawled heavily now, cradling the newborn's cold head against her own, kissing him softly. "I'm sorry baby…I'm sorry."

Shepherd tread water for a minute, holding her with one strong arm. "You did everything you could sweetheart," he sighed. "Some things aren't up to us. He was small…and vulnerable…He was like a helpless little lamb. But God has him now. He can take better care of him up there anyway...So don't cry."

But she couldn't help it. It felt as if she had lost her own child.

"Let's keep moving," Shepherd told her softly, stroking her wet hair. "We'll give the baby a proper burial, I promise.

Just then, up from the depths, two bodies burst through the water gasping for air. It was Brian and Carla, both of them breathing, both of them alive. "*Move it*!" Brian shouted, "*There's a creature in the water*!"

The group splashed with all their might, swimming hard until they reached the shore, dragging their bodies through the sand. They lay there wet and cold, breathing hard with their chests rising and falling as Sadie drew the crumpled lifeless infant to her weary chest and cried. "The baby's dead," she announced so everyone would know.

Carla burst into tears. "*No*! Why would God do this?"

"Oh, I assure you," Sadie bit back, "God did *not* do this, *I did*. *I* caused Eunice to go into labour and have the baby out here. *I* went on the Tugboat even though my gut told me not to. *I* killed this child."

"Stop it Sadie!" Brian burst out. "*You* are *not* the cause of his death. If anything, we're *all* to blame, now snap out of it. There are things going on here that we don't understand, dangerous things, and we need to pull together or we'll all end up like…like that baby and his mother."

Sadie wiped her tears, regained her composure and sat up, cradling the dead infant in her arms. "Okay then," she said, "in that case I think we ought to recognize this for what it is…and it *isn't* God. The devil is at work here tonight people, and he wants to take us out one by one. We need to pray for strength and protection."

Within minutes, Sadie led the group in prayer, all of them holding hands' taking turns praying…all except Carla.

~~~~

Why should she pray? After all, if God couldn't even protect a tiny baby, how on earth could they expect him to protect them? It made no sense at all. No, she knew when to call it quits. No God was going to rise up and rescue them now. They were all on their own.

As for the devil, he *was* a definite threat. She saw him in the water herself, and so did Brian. There was no mistaking *that*.

As the group tossed another log on the fire, they began to get warm. The roar of the flames reflected a melancholy mood after burying the infant beside his mother. It was something that had to be done, and now that it was, nobody talked about it. Instead, the conversation moved to a more tolerable discussion.

"I'll take the first watch," Brian said, "Mike and Adam are out their somewhere and if they still have ammo, we're in trouble."

"But what kind of guard will you be if you don't have a weapon to defend yourself?" Shepherd asked.

"Who says I don't have a weapon?"

Brian pulled out a gun from the back of his belted pants. He grinned in the flickering light of the fire and stuffed it back where he got it.

"Where'd you get that?" Shepherd asked.

"Ice dropped it when I tackled him. I picked it up before you came aboard. It still has a full clip."

"*All right man*! Now we got a fighting chance. I'll relieve you in four hours and take the second watch till the sun rises. I won't feel like such a helpless kitten with that thing in my belt, that's for sure."

Carla couldn't help but worry about Mike even though she knew he had caused a lot of damage, betrayed her, and run off like a fugitive. If Brian and Shepherd used the gun on Mike, she'd never forgive herself. She couldn't help it, she still loved the man.

She had to get that gun.

As the others slept around the warm fire, Carla wondered how she could possibly follow Brian to the top of the cliff where he positioned himself. It would be hard to walk that far now.

She rolled her wet pink pant leg up, revealing the wound she hid from everyone including Brian. Two red gaping holes pierced right through her ankle, just like Eunice.

Chapter 19

Pip had seen everything and he knew what it meant too: Uncle Leon was back. Who else knew he kept a tugboat he was restoring at his house? He purchased it quite a few years ago, fiddled with it until he got it working, and started using it for logging. He'd pull whatever logs he found into the logging company to make a few bucks. His plans were to restore the old relic to new condition and use it for his guiding business.

That was definitely out of the question now.

His big-mouth brothers just had to keep sending those letters to Uncle Leon when they still lived up here. They told him just about everything including the brainy ideas he had about fixing up the Tugboat. It was an ongoing joke to them, but not to Pip.

Now he had other things to worry about besides his boat burning and sinking. He and Dinah tried to get to the tip of the island when they saw the boat on fire, but it was just too far away. All they could do was hope they didn't drown.

By the time they spotted the bonfire on shore, they realized there were survivors. But who were they? It could be Uncle Leon and the treasure hunters, but he just wasn't sure until he got a little closer.

"Can we stop for a minute Pip?" Dinah panted, "My feet hurt."

"Sure," Pip answered her, sympathetic to the tiny creature. She was about half the size of him and as skinny as a rail.

"You're small…but you're pretty," he smirked at her miniature freckled face.

"That's the way God made me."

Pip felt drawn to her, he moved closer to her and wanted to kiss her but his heart just started pounding like his ancestor's drums. *Kiss the girl you fool.*

Dinah just locked eyes with him and smiled softly giving him a sideways glance. "Just kiss me you chicken," she said with a giggle, bending forward.

Rats...she's smarter than I thought.

Embarrassed, Pip leaned over to meet her lips in the middle, and held on to the kiss for a long time. It was soft, romantic, and perfect. He'd never kissed a girl before.

"I'm sorry," he said, breaking the kiss abruptly. "I-I didn't mean to."

"Yes, you did."

"I mean...I shouldn't have."

"It's okay Pip," she gazed at him softly through her big round eyes. "I've been kissed before –but never like that. It was...*nice.*"

Pip smiled shyly at her, picked up a twig, and started scratching the ground. He didn't know what to say or what to do. The stick was a much-needed distraction.

"Are you always this shy, or did God just give you too many humble genes."

"You sure talk about God a lot."

"I guess," she smiled, "Don't you?"

"No. What's there to talk about?"

"A lot," she said as she took her shoes off and started rubbing her feet.

"Like what?"

"Well, for example, the only reason I'm alive today is because of Jesus Christ. He saved me from the streets, and he's been with me ever since. I depend on him every single day of my life, like back there with that creature. You think it was a coincidence we got away? There are no coincidences. God is in control of everything. Jesus Christ is the only one that can get us off this island you know."

Pip scratched his head and looked up into the heavens. Thunder rumbled and flashes of lightning lit up the sky.

"See," Dinah said, "Like that lightning. Jesus is saying hello."

"But who is this Jesus?"

"You don't know?"

He shook his head feeling like an idiot. Grandfather and Grayling always talked about the spirits, but never once did they talk about this Jesus guy.

"I'm going to have to start from the beginning with you, aren't I?" Dinah giggled after putting her shoes back on. She pulled Pip up from where they sat and continued the conversation. "Let's get going," she said, "I'll talk while we walk."

~~~~

Dinah couldn't believe he hadn't heard about Jesus before. Hadn't everyone? Apparently not. The native population in the far north probably didn't have churches to go to, so the likelihood of hearing the gospel wasn't very high.

It was a shame really. If there were more people like Pip who didn't know a thing about the Bible, then she had her work cut out for her.

She went on explaining everything she knew, even though she didn't know very much. She had just recently become a Christian and really didn't feel qualified to teach Pip about Jesus. Where was Sadie when she needed her?

"I'm sorry," she chuckled, "I'm not exactly the best person to tell you this stuff –and it isn't even the best time to do it. Maybe I should just tell you another time."

"No –go on. It sounds interesting. What else are we going to talk about while we walk? Please...go on."

This one has open ears Lord –help my words be yours.

"O-okay," she stuttered, clearing her throat, deciding the best way to explain Christianity to him was to tell him about her own experience.

She remembered it exactly and told him every detail.

"I didn't care about anyone or anything, I just cared about the drugs. I'd do anything to get a fix at that point."

"One night I was so high, I knew I hadn't moved from the spot I was laying in for three days. My legs were numb and my clothes were dirty. I smelled like...well, let's just say I didn't exactly smell sweet. Anyway, there were others my age on the street too. Downtown east side Vancouver is like that, if you've ever been there."

"You'd think I'd know better, or at least try to get off the street, but I didn't, and nobody seemed to care that I was there. The cops would come by every now and then, and they never even bothered to ask me what my name was."

"Anyway, the next day, while I was still laying there in my own...well, you know...in filth. I knew I was coming down from a high, and needed another fix, but I couldn't get up to do anything about it. So, I started bawling, feeling like I was going to die. In a moment of weakness, I tried to pray. It's really bizarre. I didn't even know how to pray. I mumbled something about God needing to help me. That's all I can remember."

"The next thing I know, some guy bends down beside me and starts talking to me. At first, I thought he was my angel and I was in heaven...but he didn't have any wings. Then I thought he was just another john wanting me to turn a trick for him."

"Sorry Pip. Don't think less of me. That was my old life. I don't know any other way to explain what happened to me except to tell you the facts...as sick as they are."

"Anyway, it turned out that the guy was part of a group that did street ministries. He got me up and walked me to a vehicle and took me to a shelter. His church sponsored me to go to a drug rehabilitation center and I got clean."

"I still crave the drugs everyday, but God helps me with that one *big-time*."

"Then they sent me to Shining Star and I met Sadie. She told me the rehab center cleaned up my body from the drugs, but Jesus could clean my soul."

"It sounds like a bunch of malarkey, I know. At first, I thought it was, but then it made sense. I didn't have people in my life that cared about me. My mom was never around, and when she was, she'd have a different guy every day of the week. I called a lot of guys daddy, but they were everything *but* my daddy...if you know what I mean. See, I didn't have anyone in my life to rescue me. I was all alone in the world with nowhere to turn. But Sadie said I could have a friend that would rescue me and never take advantage of me, or leave me alone to die on the streets like my mother did when she finally kicked me out of the house because I told her daddy number 25 was abusing me."

"I wanted to be accepted and loved. I wanted someone to forgive me for the rotten things I did in my life. I needed that forgiveness so I could start my life over. All I did was pray a simple prayer with Sadie and all my sins just melted away."

"But I had to believe in Jesus *forever*, and not only that...I had to leave my sinful ways behind. And you know what? You'd think that would be a drag, but it wasn't. I actually *wanted* to change. There was nothing that I felt I *had* to give up. I *wanted* to give my old life up. It's hard to explain."

Pip stood there stunned when she finished. He didn't say a word. The tears in his eyes said it all.

"Pip? she said, "Are you okay?"

He shook his head. "I'm lonely too," he whispered. "Can *I* have what you have?"

"Sure, you can," she answered him, unable to see him clearly with all the tears flooding her eyes. "All you have to do is pray this prayer with me."

The two of them turned to each other, held hands, and looked into each other's teary eyes. Dinah told him to repeat after her, and he did. They prayed a prayer that had changed Dinah's life forever and brought Jesus to live in her heart as her savior. Now the same thing was happening to Pip and it gave her goose bumps all over.

Thank you, Jesus!

"Am I different?" Pip chided as they both finished the prayer.

"What do *you* think?"

"I feel...kind of strange, like that lightning up there went straight through me."

Dinah wanted to giggle, but she refrained herself. He was so much like a child –innocent with his belief. "That would be the Holy Spirit. Remember I told you about him when we first started this conversation. He's your promised helper –the spirit of God. Just remember what I said about the egg and you won't get confused. An egg has three parts, the yoke, the white, and the shell, but we still call it one egg, right? That's the way God is. He has three parts too –The father, the Son, and the Holy Spirit. We still call him God though, or Lord. Do you get it?"

"I sure do," he answered back, sniffling a bit. "My Grandfather couldn't have explained it any better, and he was the best storyteller around."

But their conversation was interrupted by a noise in the pine trees just ahead of them. "Did you hear that?" Pip asked suddenly.

Dinah's eyes grew wide. "Somebody's coming," she whispered.

Chapter 20

Pip and Dinah ducked behind a rock but nobody came their way. Maybe they were just being paranoid. The monster had given them a good scare and they hadn't seen him in a while. But then Uncle Leon was somewhere on Reefers Island, and so were the others. That alone sent shivers up his spine.

"Let's go," he told Dinah, "We were just hearing things."

But in his heart, he knew something was out there watching them, and it wasn't just God, it was something evil.

Hey there Jesus...it's the new kid. I wonder if you could help us out. Not so much for me, but if you could make sure Dinah is safe, I would really appreciate it.

The two of them couldn't stay there any longer, it was starting to rain and the slope down to the campfire would be slippery. The sooner they got down from the cliff they were on, the better.

"Here, give me your hand and I'll help you down," he said, wiping the sprinkles from his face. "These rocks get a little slick when it rains."

As Pip helped Dinah down from a boulder, they both suddenly froze. Someone was definitely in the bush ahead of them. Clapping sounds reverberated through the trees.

"Who's there?" Pip shouted, swinging Dinah behind him to protect her.

Then someone laughed.

"Reveal yourself, you coward."

Then from behind a huge pine tree a dark figure emerged clapping and laughing like he was sure of himself.

"Bravo! That was a pretty heart-warming conversation I heard the two of you have Pippi Longstocking. It made me think I was watching a soap opera. I didn't know your little girly friend had such a colorful past. Hey babe, maybe you and I should hook up sometime…Like right now."

Pip knew the voice, there was no mistaking it even in the dark. "Don't come any closer Mike," Pip shouted, bending down to pick up a pointy twig. It wasn't a sword but it would do just the same.

"What –are you going to use your magic wand on me Pippy?" Mike laughed. "You better watch out, you might conjure up the boogie man and you wouldn't want that. You know how creepy he is with those yellow eyes of his."

"Shut up!"

"Oh, big man in front of the princess, but don't think you scare me. I got reinforcements you know."

Pip spun his head around like a top. Suddenly three men appeared holding guns at them. *This would be a good time for that help I asked for Jesus.*

"Don't let them get me Pip," Dinah sobbed into his back as she stuck to him like glue. He reached his arm behind him and patted her on her hip. "I won't."

"Oh, isn't that *cute*," Mike mocked, "Pippi Longstocking has a girly friend."

"What do you want with us?"

Then a familiar voice spoke like an eerie ghost, mechanical and cold. "The girl knows what I want."

"Uncle Leon?"

Lightning lit up the sky just enough so he and Dinah could get a good glimpse of who this was for sure. Dinah gasped, and Pip growled, "*Leave us alone!*"

"Shut up *Pipata*…and hand over Amanda."

~~~

Brian thought he heard voices, but the thunder was getting louder and it drowned it out. Now he didn't know what direction to search. The intermittent rain and the lack of light didn't make it any easier.

You're the light unto my path Lord…Lead the way.

For a moment he listened again, trying to hear beyond the pitter-patter of raindrops on the leaves around him. *That was definitely a scream.*

Bolting like the lightning above, Brian took off through the bush, due north up to the higher cliff above.

~~~

Carla waited for Shepherd and Sadie to fall asleep before she made her exit. She wrapped her ankle with a tensor bandage and it didn't feel as bad as she thought it would feel to walk on it. Maybe it was already healing. That would be a relief considering her worst fears were that it would become infected like it did for Eunice.

Hobbling a bit, she set off up the slope into the pine forest where she saw Brian take off too. The rain didn't deter her one bit. In fact, she was use to it from being out in the boat all week. The weather wasn't exactly co-operative.

For a long time now, Carla had wanted to go on a hike like this, she just didn't think it would be in the middle of the night stranded on a remote island in Northern Saskatchewan. The circumstances weren't exactly ideal.

If she could only find Brian sleeping, and take the gun from his hand, the whole thing would be a lot easier. But that wasn't likely. He was a trained professional, and she wasn't.

Thunder rumbled above her, sending a chill up her spin as she cautiously moved through the leafy terrain. It was hard to see, but she had to go on. If Brian used that gun on Mike, she'd never have a chance to find out what went on back there at the boat.

It wasn't like him to do such a thing. Mike was wild but he wasn't a killer. He wouldn't shoot anyone. At least she hoped he wouldn't. She hadn't known him very long, but what she did know of him was that he had a gentle side. *Or was that fake too.*

Either he loved her or he didn't. That was the question. From what Ice said to her in the boat, it sounded like Mike was just using her, but that couldn't be. The intimate moments they shared together were so genuine.

With another clash of thunder, Carla jumped. Rain speckled her face as she looked up to the lightning high in the sky. This storm could get worse, and she'd be stuck in the bush. That didn't bode well for her. She'd have to find Brian quickly. Maybe she could sweet-talk him into giving her the gun. It worked for most men, but one thing she had discovered already was that Brian wasn't like most men.

Usually she could get away with her flirting, but sometimes she couldn't, like the time she poured it on so the pastor would let her lead the Sunday School Christmas program. It was a church she attended when her second child was only five years old. Pastor Donald didn't know what hit him, but his wife sure did. She was furious...but that just fuelled the fire.

"If you don't leave my husband alone," Mrs. Donald scolded her, "I'll have to do something drastic."

"Oh yah," Carla snapped back in a heated discussion in the church library. "What might that be?"

"I'll bring it up at the next board meeting."

"You do that!"

Carla didn't think she really would, but a few weeks before Christmas, just when the Christmas program was starting to come together, she got a phone call from her. "The board would like to meet with you tomorrow evening Carla," Mrs. Donald told her on the phone. "And you'd better be there."

"What if I'm not?"

"Just be there!" the woman shouted, slamming the phone in her ear.

The nerve of some people. And they call themselves Christians. How could a pastor's wife be so nasty to her? She was just mad that she took over the Christmas program that use to be her domain. It didn't have anything to do with flirting with Pastor Donald.

At the board meeting the next evening, Carla was prepared to go in there fighting. Instead, she barely said a word...the board wouldn't let her. "Mrs Reece," one of them said to her, "Please stand up when we're speaking to you."

Carla could see Mrs. Donald's glaring eyes laughing at her, spiteful as ever. If this was Christianity, she didn't want any part of it.

"We as a board wish to inform you that you and your family are no longer welcome at this church. We have already voted and it's unanimous. We know what kind of woman you are, and we won't have it in our church. Please leave immediately."

Carla felt tears filling her eyes. "That's it?" she sobbed like a fool. "I don't get to say anything? Your going to convict me without the decency of a trial even?"

"You already said plenty...to me," the pastors wife grinned, "I told them what you said."

I'll bet you did.

Carla remembered the emotional hour that followed. She ripped down all the artwork she had put up for the backdrop of the play, and cut up the costumes she worked so hard on...And Mrs. Donald couldn't stop her.

One more church down the toilet.

After that, Carla just gave up on churches altogether, only going at Christmas and Easter, and only to the larger churches, the ones where she would be lost in the crowd and nobody could judge her.

John took the kids though...every Sunday to a very small Pentecostal church down the street from them. Carla didn't want anything to do with them. Never again would she invest *anything*, not her money or her time, in a church with so called *Christian* people. They were all hypocrites as far as she was concerned.

And the flirting...it just continued.

Carla learned to use her body as a weapon, a powerful weapon. If those church people thought they knew what kind of woman she was, they hadn't seen the half of it. She figured if everyone already had her pegged as some harlot...Why try to fight it?   Yes, she could seduce the devil and get away with it.

Thunder clashed above her as a large tree branch slapped her in the face. It woke her from her disturbing memory, making the rage she kept inside of her subside a bit.

Yes, she would definitely try to seduce Brian into giving her the gun. It would work...It had always worked.

As the rain started to pour now, Carla's hair stuck to her face. It had dried as she sat around the fire, but now it was wet again. She always looked better with wet hair, sexy and sultry. She smoothed it around her face.

With both hands she ripped open the collar of her wet pink sweat suit right down to her implants. She drew the bottom of her sweatshirt together, wringing it out a bit and then she tied it in a knot right under her breasts like a halter top revealing her perfectly tanned tummy tuck, exposed to the romantic lightning flickering in the night sky.

Perfect.

Now she was ready for battle. No man could resist her, not even the straight-laced Brian, and his *I'm a perfect Christian* charade. She'd known men like him before, many of them, and they were *always* breakable.

All she had to do was find him now.

The rain became more intense as Carla searched the bush in the dark. She peered around huge boulders and large pine trees, but Brian was nowhere to be found. *Could he have gone back to camp?*

Then from behind a clump of trees, she saw something moving. "Brian?", she said, hoping she had finally found him.

No answer.

The rain could drown out most sounds but surely, he could hear her, she was close enough to him. "Brian?" she asked again, "Is that you?"

A low earthy growl assaulted the night.

Chapter 21

"Her name isn't *Amanda!*" Pip fumed, furious at his uncle's insinuation that he knew Dinah when he didn't.

Dinah shook as she clung to Pip. She didn't say a word.

"Are you going to tell him sweet cheeks, or should I," Leon retorted with a sly grin as if he had a big secret.

Pip backed up with Dinah still behind him. "Don't answer that," he told her. "My uncle thinks he owns *everybody.*"

"Oh, but I *do* own *her*, she's *all* mine."

"Over my dead body!"

"If you insist," Leon smirked, rushing up to Pip, thrusting the gun to his temple. "This brings back memories doesn't it kid?"

"Stop!" Dinah finally spoke, pulling away from Pip, standing on her own now.

Leon grabbed Pip around the neck and dragged him away from Dinah, still with the gun to his temple. He could hardly breath.

The other two guys just stood their and laughed.

"You win Leon," Dinah sobbed, "I'll tell him."

Betrayal stung the air as Pip lifted his head and listened to her. His eyes began to tear even before she said a word.

"I know him Pip. I-I didn't know he was your uncle and I haven't seen him in a while. Honestly, it's been a long time."

Leon released his grip on Pip, lowering the gun from his temple to the middle of his back. "Not that long honey, I still have the taste of you in my mouth and I miss you baby," he said licking his lips like a dirty pig.

Dinah burst into tears and covered her face with her hands.

"Oh, don't be bashful. Did you tell him I was your *first*? How old were you then, thirteen? It was right before I came out here the last time, when you started working for me, remember? Lucky, I did time in Vancouver so I could keep an eye on you. Haven't seen you since they sent me to the P.A Pen. though. Looks like you been busy."

Pip's stomach churned. He gagged, bringing up his stomach contents inches away from Leon's foot. His uncle smacked him in the head with the gun, sending him careening into his own vomit. Dinah sobbed as she rushed up to him, grabbing hold of his arm to help him up.

Pip shoved her away. He didn't know why, he just did, and it made him even sicker. All he could see were her big round eyes shocked and hurt. She hung her head and backed away from him, sobbing profusely.

"See Pip," Leon spit, "I told you she was mine."

"You sick freak!" Pip moaned and held his head.

Leon kicked him in the stomach this time, and he recoiled like a caterpillar.

"Come to Daddy baby," Leon smiled, holding his arms out to her. But she turned her head away from him and didn't move.

"Daddy has some candy for his baby, just like old times," he told her, reaching into his pocket pulling out a sealed bag of white powder and dangling it in front of her.

"I don't do that anymore," Dinah sniffled and hiccupped, wiping her nose with her sleeve, glancing at Pip one more time.

"Don't look at *him*," Leon grinned, "He's not going to save you, you know. He don't want *soiled* goods. I'm the only one who cares about you baby. *I'm* your Daddy, I'll give you what you need, now come here before I put a bullet through Pipata's head."

Pip tried to speak, but nothing would come out. He wanted to tell her to run, to never look back, but the words wouldn't form properly in his mouth. *What's the matter with me?*

Then, Adam and Mike rushed up to her and shoved her into Leon's arms before she even had a chance to run. "I'm gonna like this," Mike beamed.

"Shut up Mike," Leon reprimanded him. "Nobody touches the girl till we're done the job. You hear me? First, I need a fix, and so does she. Then we head for the caves."

"But I told you, Cutter blew them all up," Mike said.

"Not those caves you moron, the ones right here on the island. That's where the mother load is."

"What do we do with Pippi Longstocking?" Mike asked.

"Leave him for the python."

~~~~

The showers had stopped for the time being. Brian was glad for that because it slowed him down. He had to step so carefully or else he'd slip on the mossy rocks that planted themselves everywhere.

It seemed like he'd been walking in circles for the last half hour because he kept passing the same old rotten tree trunk, or was it a different one this time? He didn't know for sure. It was so hard to track someone in the dark. Brian wasn't cut out for this. It reminded him of the Shooting Star incident, and it felt the same too.

Finally, Brian heard noises again, telling him he was going the right direction after all. This time it sounded like someone was moaning, and it was coming from that large boulder up ahead.

He ran through the tree branches slapping at him like a large broom. When he arrived at the rock, someone lay there on the ground moaning. He steadied his gun and approached with caution.

"Who's there?" he asked, swallowing hard as he focused his eyes in the night. But all that answered him was the same moaning sound as before.

Brian inched forward slowly with apprehension in his gait. Then, there on the ground he approached a body curled up in the fetal position, obviously wounded. "Are you okay?" he asked the native male, turning him over to see his face.

"Pip? Is that you?"

Memories flooded back to him of a curious young thirteen-year-old boy named Pipata who saved his life and the lives of his friends five years ago during the Shooting Star incident. It was a memory locked in time, but not forgotten. And now here he was all grown up and still in just as much trouble as ever. Actually, this boy had more guts than most men, and wisdom beyond his years.

"Brian?" the boy moaned, holding his head up.

"What happened here?"

Pip told him about the guiding job he'd been hired for. He told him about Mike, and Adam, and how they turned on him. Then he told him about his uncle and that shocked him. How on earth did he get free from the rope when they went in to the water. Any normal person would have drowned in the water with his arms and legs tied up. Was Leon Houdini or something?

"Come on," Brian said, "Let's get you up. I'll take you back to our camp and get you warm. We have a medical kit there."

"No," Pip moaned as he stood. "I have to find someone."

"You're in no shape to be traipsing around in the middle of the night. It's wet, it's cold, and it's dangerous."

"I'm not thirteen anymore either."

"No, you're not Pip."

"Then let me go. I have to go after someone…She's in trouble."

Pip told him about Dinah and what happened before he got there. Then he told him about the caves. "Do you know where they are?" Brian asked.

"No, that's the thing. I've never heard of any caves right here on Reefers Island. I knew of some underwater a few miles from shore, but they're gone now. Obviously, Uncle Leon knows where they are, and he went west."

"Then let's go west."

~~~~

It was a baby *creature* of some kind.

Carla had been almost frightened to death, but the thing was actually harmless. She tried to pick it up but it wouldn't let her. It looked like a cross between a snake and a baby seal pup, and had webbed feet. It's eyes were yellow like cat eyes.

Could this have been what she had seen in the water? It couldn't be. How could such a small thing leave such big teeth marks in her ankle. This creature had sharp pointy teeth but they were very small.

The creature hissed and drew back from her, it scurried around and took off. Carla followed it to a large outcrop of rocks straight ahead, and noticed it disappeared.

Did it go in there?

In front of her stood an opening to what appeared to be an old mine shaft. The creature went this way, so Carla would too. It was fascinating. She'd never seen anything like it.

"Come here little guy," she said, stepping carefully. She couldn't see a thing. Instead of turning around to find her way back out, she realized she had better stay put and get her bearings first. The entrance was no longer visible.

Then she heard a hissing sound again and decided to blindly follow, figuring he could see better in the dark than she could.

Step by step Carla continued on, noticing a strange smell in the air. It was nauseating, and made it hard to breath. She could tell she was walking on a slant, declining deeper and deeper into the mine shaft.

Another hissing sound echoed in the distance, this time further away than before. There was no way she was going to find that thing now. It was too fast and had an advantage being able to see in the dark.

Never before had Carla been so frightened and alone. She decided to sit tight and wait for it to come back this way and lead her out. *This must be what it's like being blind.* She couldn't even see her hand in front of her face.

As she sat there, the quietness of the tunnel just gave her the creeps. All she could hear was the sound of dripping water. It was an eerie feeling being completely helpless in the dark. Why had she gone in there? She was supposed to be looking for Brian…seducing him into giving her the gun, not sitting helpless in some kind of tunnel.

After some time had passed and Carla's butt was getting pretty sore, she wondered what it would be like if she were Sadie. That woman had the kind of faith she'd been after all her life. If she were here, she'd probably be leading a Bible study right now, or praying.

Praying. Carla wished she had the proper words to say a prayer right now. She couldn't even remember the ones she used to say when she was a child. In fact, so much time had lapsed since her last prayer, she almost didn't know *how* to pray any more.

She scratched her head and tried anyway. "Lord hear my prayer…The Father, Son, and Holy Ghost…Hallowed be thy name forever and ever…. *Oh, forget it.*"

This was not working. Sadie's prayers didn't sound like this. They weren't so formal, or forced. Why was it every time she tried to pray lately, it sounded like a foreign language?

Maybe it just wasn't' meant to be? Maybe communicating with God really was meant for only the priests…and women like Sadie.

As Carla sat there still and alone, she thought of what had been going on in her life. Was she happy with the choices she had made? Was she content with the way she had lived her life so far? If she was honest with herself, she would have to say no. She wished she could have been that perfect Christian everyone expected her to be.

If only she had done things differently. If only she had been stronger. "I want to be better God," she said surprising herself. *I think that was just a prayer.*

Maybe there was hope for her after all?

Then, from somewhere in the distance, Carla heard voices. At first, she wanted to yell out to them so they could rescue her, but then she thought twice about it. She would find out who it was first.

A few feet in front of her, she saw a flickering light. *They have flashlights.* Then they came closer and she hid behind a large boulder tucked away in a corner. They started talking.

"You might not think so," a loud obnoxious voice said to the others, "but this place is filled with diamonds.

"Would you make a ring for me Daddy," a juvenile female voice giggled as if she were drunk. "I want to marry you baby."

Carla wondered who on earth *that* was. She peeked over the top of the rock and got a glimpse of the silly little blonde hanging on the big Indian's arm as if he were her idol. *What the...*

Didn't Ice drown? And that was Dinah. What did she think she was doing? Carla had never heard the petite freckled blonde talk like this.

"Come on Ice," Mike jigged up and down like a little kid. "Can't I have some fun with the girl first. Please!"

Carla's heart skipped a beat when she heard that. She wanted to jump up right then and there, and slap his dirty face. But she didn't. Something told her to keep listening.

"I thought you liked old ladies?" Ice snapped back with a laugh.

"And wrinkles," Adam added.

I don't have wrinkles.

"Carla was just...for kicks," Mike told them. "All I wanted was her money, you guys know that. She was the ugliest witch I ever slept with."

Tears formed in her eyes. His words stung like a dagger that had just sliced through her skin. How could he say such a thing? How could she be so stupid? It *was* true. He had used her for her money and she fell for it.

Dinah giggled and danced around losing her balance, falling on the ground snorting swear words so colorful Carla wouldn't even say them. "Oops," the girl laughed, "I-I don't know what's wrong with me. I just feel so...*good*."

Carla could see desire in Mike's eyes and it made her sick. She knew that look all too well. "Come on Ice," he begged, "let me have some fun with her. She's asking for it and everything."

As Carla watched with wide eyes, hopeful Mike wouldn't get his wish, she felt her face heat up. *Jesus...do not let this happen.*

"Come on Ice," Mike begged again. "*Pretty please!*"

"Fine," Ice agreed, "but you owe me big...and you only have five minutes."

Carla couldn't stand it anymore. She jumped right up and shouted, "*NO!*" before she even thought it through. There was no way she was letting this happen.

"Well, well, well," Mike snickered, "speak of the devil."

"You're not touching her Mike!" Carla said almost bawling.

"He can do whatever he wants you *old bag*," Dinah spit, "you're not his *mother*. But then again...Maybe you are?" she snorted and giggled at what she said, swearing at Carla with the foulest of words.

"Go get your old lady Mike," Ice said impatiently. "I had enough of this."

"But what about the girl?"

"Forget it," Ice said, "I changed my mind. If you're stupid bimbo could find us, then the others might too. We have to get a move on."

"Oh, come on…"

"I don't care Mike," Ice growled, "We don't got time for this. Tie the women up and leave them here till we get back. We gotta go deeper to find the rocks and I don't feel like dragging *them* with us. We'll deal with them after. Got it?"

"Got it!"

Chapter 22

Shepherd woke with a start.

It was almost time to relieve Brian. He'd throw a few more logs on the fire for the women and then go find Brian. But then he noticed Carla was missing.

"Carla?" he called out, trying not to wake Sadie.

"What is it Shepherd? Sadie groaned, waking from her sleep.

Waking her was the last thing he wanted to do, but under the circumstances, maybe it was good. "I can't find Carla," he said. "Do you know where she went?"

"Bathroom probably."

"You better hope so because I've got to go and relieve Brian right now."

"*Carla*!" they both shouted cupping their hands around their mouths. If anything, she was out of earshot. The rain had stopped and everything sounded hollow, but even still, if she went a ways to find a private spot to relieve herself, she might not hear them.

"I'll wait for a few more minutes, then I'm going to look for her."

"I'm not staying here all by myself."

Shepherd sighed. Bringing her with him was not the safest plan, but neither was leaving her alone. "I'll go get Brian and send him right back here. Maybe by then Carla will be back. You'll only be alone for a few minutes...ten tops."

"I don't care. I'm coming with you to get Brian."

Shepherd sighed. How could he say no to a charming woman like Sadie? After all, he was responsible for her and leaving her alone wasn't exactly responsible. "Okay, but stay close to me.

Who knows what might be lurking in that dark bush?"

The two of them waited as long as they could but Carla still didn't return. Shepherd shrugged and held out his hand to the lady. "Time to go."

~~~~

Trudging through the wilderness wasn't exactly what Sadie would call a perfect first date, but it felt like it. Shepherd was all gentlemanly with her. It made her feel secure, protected from whatever was out there.

Not in a million years did she think she would feel like this again. The last time her stomach did somersaults for any man was when she was still in college, and her studies always got in the way. Then it was her career.

If she had met someone like Shepherd back then, would it have gotten her mind off teaching? Probably not, but it was a good thought. She wondered what her life would have been like if she would have married and started a family like all of her friends. Yet, the Lord had blessed her in her singleness. And it was a good life so far.

Him holding her hand right now felt like a good life too. *Why didn't I marry?* It was a hard question. Perhaps she thought it was too late. Perhaps it *was* too late.

"Can I ask you a question?" he asked.

"You sure can."

"When we get out of here," he said apprehensively, "and I know we will because God will see us through this."

"Definitely!" she replied, hoping that was the case, but knowing God didn't always work that way. Our plans were not always the Lords plans. That was a fact that most people didn't quite understand. Not even her. Losing Eunice and the baby was a perfect example of that. All she knew was that God knows what he's doing.

Shepherd continued shakily as if he were trying to pop the question. "W-when we get out of here, do you think we can start going out. I-I mean, could I take you out on a date sometime. I would really like to. I think you're a w-wonderful woman."

Sadie stopped for a moment and looked him squarely in the eyes. "You know I run Shining Star Lodge, don't you?"

"I do."

"How can we date when you don't live here?"

"I'll rent a room in your lodge for a while."

Sadie grinned and lowered her head. "Oh, I don't know...perhaps, as long as I have guests living there, I guess. I wouldn't want people to talk."

"Let them."

Sadie felt her face blushing. If it was daytime instead of night, he might actually see it too. "You're embarrassing me."

"Good!"

This guy was a little too forward, but she liked it. For the first time in a long time, he made her feel like there might be wedding bells in her future after all.

"Well," he said, "What do you say? Would you date an old jailbird like me?"

"I might just do that. But first, we have to get off this island."

"Right," he grinned, continuing the walk, squeezing her hand as she tried to keep up to his big strides. "Let's try calling for Carla again."

The two of them shouted for long periods of time, listening to nothing but the echo answer them back.

"I don't know what could have happened to her," Sadie said. "Do you think she might have gone off to find her boyfriend?"

"Maybe," Shepherd said, shushing her. "Did you hear that?"

"No."

"Listen. I thought I heard someone calling back to us.

He called out for Carla and then listened, putting his finger over his mouth to quiet her. "It's Brian," he smiled. "Thank the good Lord. I told you God has our back."

As she and Shepherd met up with Brian, they discovered someone else was with him. "Shepherd," Brian introduced him, "this is Pipata Eaglefeather, better known as Pip. He helped us solve the Shooting Star case back five years ago.

"Pleased to meet you," Shepherd said, shaking the tall teenagers hand.

"I've already met you son," Sadie nodded. "I didn't know who you were though. I thought you were running with those treasure hunters." He looked like he had too, his body had obviously taken some kind of beating.

"They just hired me as the guide," Pip told her. "I had to stay at the lodge with them. That was the deal I made."

"You didn't tell me he was staying at the lodge," Brian piped up. "You should have told me Sadie."

"Like I said, I didn't exactly know who he was."

Brian looked a little perturbed with her. It was probably just fatigue. She *did* worry about him though. This scenario had to bring back bad memories. She knew he had a hard time dealing with what happened here five years ago. "Are you okay Brian?" she asked him. "You sound…stressed."

"Who wouldn't be under these circumstances."

Brian filled her and Shepherd in on what was going on, and they informed him that Carla was missing. Their plan was to find the caves and go after Mike and his gang, but they didn't want her to come along.

"I'm going with you!"

"No, you're not," Brian insisted. "I don't want to be responsible for you."

"Nothing will happen to me, I'll stick with Shepherd."

Sadie smiled at Shepherd expecting his accepting eyes to agree with her but they didn't. "He's right Sadie, it's too dangerous for you. You should wait for Carla back at the campfire."

It was hard to contain herself. Tears began to flood her eyes.

"Come on you guys," Pip butt in, "We have to find Dinah before they hurt her."

"*What?*" Did she just hear what she thought she heard? Do they know where *Dinah* is? "*Where's my butterfly*? You tell me where my butterfly is!"

"Thanks a lot Pip," Brian groaned. "I told you not to say anything."

Pip just shrugged.

"Don't you scold him Brian Mackie. You tell me where Dinah is right now, and you better tell me everything."

Brian made Pip tell her the short version of the story, and Sadie's knees buckled as she fell to the ground sobbing. Shepherd put his hand on her shoulder and knelt down beside her. "That's why you can't come with us," he told her, trying to comfort her. "It's just not safe."

Sadie wiped her nose with the back of her hand and stood up. "Not even a million dollars would make me stay behind. I'm going to save my butterfly whether you *men* like it or not. *She needs me*! There are just some things that women do better than men, and if she's been...*attacked*, she needs me all the more. *Now let's get going!*"

The men all eyed each other and didn't say a word. Her mother hen instinct had kicked into overdrive whether it was sensible or not.

Lord God Almighty, please protect that precious child!

~~~~

Brian was glad that Pip kept quiet about Leon offering Dinah the drugs. If he would have let that slip, who knows what Sadie would have done. The woman wasn't exactly thinking straight. As far as Brian was concerned, it was dangerous for her, *and* for them. There really was no way of knowing what was going on down there in those caves even though Pip told him they were after diamonds...*again.*

Leon was after stolen diamonds five years ago too. But this time they wanted to mine them. Nothing criminal in that, he supposed, just the means in which they wanted to go about doing it.

It didn't make much sense. Why did they have to hurt people in the process? *Once a con always a con,* he guessed. They didn't know any other way to get what they wanted. That didn't say much for Shepherd, though he said he had made definite changes in his life while still in prison. Still, did he really know the man he was travelling with, and why did he let Sadie get so close to him? He could be in on this whole thing.

"Sadie, why don't you walk up her with me for a while," he said, looking at Shepherd, still holding her hand and helping her walk every step in the dark. Maybe he shouldn't be paranoid, but at this point, he didn't really know what was going on or who to trust.

"I'm fine back here with Shepherd," she answered him.

"No!" Brian replied louder than he intended. "*I want you up here with me.*"

Shepherd stopped for moment, holding up the group once again. "Wait a minute Brian. Are you trying to insinuate the lady isn't safe with me? Is that it? You think I've got something to do with this whole thing just because I'm a con?"

Busted. Now he had to fess up. "Well, do you?"

"Of course not!"

"Well, you know Ice, and…"

"And you think just because I spent time in prison with him, he and I are in cahoots with each other. Is that right? You think we planned this whole thing…what, for the fun of it? *Man,* I told you I gave my life to Jesus, doesn't that matter to you."

Now Brian felt bad, he shouldn't have judged the burly tattooed man. He may be from a rough background, but that didn't mean he was double-crossing him. Perhaps not all cons were the same after all.

"I'm sorry brother," he told Shepherd. "Lets just keep moving, we're all getting a little island crazy. But in the back of his mind, he'd still keep an eye out for their new friend. Things weren't always as they seemed.

Shepherd sighed, accepted Brian's apology, and continued on without a word.

Pip trudged off ahead of everyone, obviously eager to get to the caves. Brian sped up to him hoping to talk to him, leaving the fuming Shepherd and Sadie further back. It was good he kept his distance from the two of them for a while.

"Wait up Pip," Brian called out to the native teen. "Can I ask you a question?"

"I guess."

"What's your take on the big guy back there. I mean, have you ever seen him up here before, or with your uncle?"

"Never. I thought you two were friends."

"Well sort of." Brian scratched his head and looked back in Shepherd and Sadie's direction, hearing them moving through the bushy terrain. "I just want to be sure he's a trustworthy guy, that's all. I want to know we're all on the same side."

Pip turned his head annoyed. "He *said* he gave his life to *Jesus.*"

Brian wondered what Pip would know about that. "…and your point is?"

"Any friend of Jesus is a friend of mine."

The boy couldn't possibly know what he was talking about. Native people that lived way up north knew nothing of white culture. They only knew of their own Indian legends and worshiped their ancestors and spirits, not usually *Jesus Christ.* "A lot of people say they're Christians, but they're not Pip. Most people don't even know what a Christian is. Do you?"

"I don't know what *Christian* means. I've never heard of it before."

"My point exactly. Now why don't you just take my word for it. Some people put on an act. I think Shepherd might be one of them. I might be wrong, but will you help me? Will you help me keep an eye on him? You and I have history together. I know your ways, and you know mine. We trust each other. That's why I need your help when we get to the caves. Can I count on you?"

Pip looked at him for a minute, then turned back at Shepherd and Sadie. "You can count on me."

Chapter 23

In the damp foul smelling cave, Carla could see the glowing eyes. The small creature was back. "Come here little fella," she whispered trying not to wake Dinah who had passed out an hour ago shortly after the men took off.

The small creature approached them, licking Carla's bound hands. "Yah, that's right little guy," she said, "bite the rope for me."

If she could get him to use his sharp teeth to cut through the rope, they might actually have a chance. But he seemed to be more interested in her ankle. The wounded one. It whimpered beside her like a crying baby, now starting to lick the foot that seemed to be covered in puss.

She hadn't even noticed it until now, but she winced in pain as the creature started biting at her toes. "*Get!*" she said, kicking at the thing the best she could wile having both her feet tied up.

In complete darkness, it was hard to figure what the little beast would do next. She felt him brush by her head now, sniffing, going for her neck.

She let out a frantic scream –it drew back.

This creature reminded her of a sewer rat, the way it kept biting at her. And the noise that came from it sent shivers up her spine. It grew louder and louder like it was calling something. Surely Dinah couldn't sleep through *this*, most people couldn't. But then she wasn't *most* people, she wasn't even the little *nice* girl Carla thought she was.

Yes, Dinah had fooled them all.

There it went again, licking her festering ankle. "Come on," she moaned, "*leave me alone*!" Why did it have to do that to her? It wasn't bothering Dinah at all.

Carla picked up a rock with both hands bound and threw it at the creature, sending it into a panic as it squealed and scurried away.

That serves you right you varmint.

Within moments, Carla realized it wasn't coming back. Perhaps the thing was gone for good. Maybe now she could calm down some, and actually think of a way to get out of here. She'd have to come up with something on her own, Dinah obviously wasn't going to be much help.

Then from the corner of her eye, she saw the yellow slanted eyes glowing again. This time they were bigger, about the same size as the ones she saw in the water.

Oh no, Mamma and baby!

Carla moaned, pulling at her bound hands trying to break free –but the eyes kept coming at her, hissing with a low earthy growl that sent echoes through the cave.

She could feel the larger creature's warm breath on her neck as the yellow eyes danced around her, sniffing her, smelling her as if considering her for a meal for herself and the little one.

"Don't move!" a voice suddenly shot out in the dark, holding a flashlight at the entrance to the cave. It was Brian and Shepherd and that Indian guide.

The creature retreated from Carla and slid it's enormous black shiny body over to the group, sniffing them as they stood like statues against this thing.

The light revealed the enormity of the foul creature, about the same size as a pre-historic dinosaur. It's face looked like the head of a serpent with a body like that of a fish of some kind.

Carla tried not to make a sound, quieting her breathing as if she were holding her breath. *This is the thing...this is the thing that bit me in the water.* But of course, they didn't know it had bitten her at all.

As the beast slinked around the people, hissing and observing, it stopped at the native boy and hovered there, growling now and bearing it's teeth. The native boy said nothing. He closed his eyes as if he were wishing the thing to go away.

Slime dripped from it's mouth as it now moved over to Dinah, still laying there in her slumber. He sniffed around her body and turned away quickly. The baby scurried around Carla's feet again, licking her festering ankle. She shook in terror as the mother approached her now.

Be still...Be still and know that I am God.

It was the only thing that came to mind, the only thing that fit. The mother began licking at Carla's ankle too, tugging and lapping until her foot turned numb.

"S-someone pray for me," she sobbed ever so softly, hoping they heard her, hoping the beast *didn't*.

The others slowly moved toward her, even Sadie now. They stopped and started every time the creature turned its head, as if they were playing red light green light. But the creature continued licking her ankle. "W-what's it doing?" Carla sobbed, moaning through her throat. "*I-is he...e-eating me?*"

It was as if the monster didn't even know they were there now. It focused solely on the task apparently unaware of anything else. Baby and mamma were busy feasting.

"Pray with me Sadie," Carla moaned. "I don't want to die like this. Tell me what I should pray. I'm ready to repent. I don't want to go to hell."

"Carla," Sadie whispered as she cautiously approached Dinah, kneeling down beside her. "Just stay quiet."

"No, I'm gonna die, *please,* tell me what I should pray before it's too late."

"Not now…this isn't the time or the place."

The creature stopped for a moment, looked around curiously and continued licking the festering puss from Carla's numb foot.

"*Please*…I don't want to go to hell!"

"Okay, but…" Sadie continued with a shaky voice, "you have to repeat these words –*I accept Jesus Christ as my personal savior with all of my heart.*"

Carla stared at her with big round serious eyes and repeated every word.

"I repent of my sinful lifestyle and all the sin I've chosen to live with."

She repeated that too.

"By faith I accept Christ's mercy and forgiveness which he bought for me on the cross of Calvary."

Carla hesitated first…then whispered that as well.

"With the help and power of the Holy Spirit, I want to be a faithful follower of Christ from this day forward."

She sobbed as she repeated this part.

"And do you mean it with all your heart? – because they're just words if you don't mean it Carla."

For the first time in her life, Carla *really* meant it. She was ready to die. Sadie risked her own life to make sure of that. Tears welled up in her throat and in her eyes that she couldn't express. "I mean it with *all* my heart."

"Now…try to pull your foot away from the monster."

What? That wasn't what she expected her to say. "But I can't," Carla bawled now, knowing that would mean *certain* death.

"You must!"

Every trembling nerve in her body told her not to, but her heart kept telling her she had to at least try. Then, swallowing hard, she pulled her still bound feet from the monster's jaws, sending it into a wild screaming fit as if it were being tortured.

Brain and the Indian guide dragged her body into the corner and set her down beside Dinah. Mother and baby beast continued with the horrible screeching as if they were calling someone or *something*.

"That's the calling sound," Carla told them, panting out of breath as she watched the monsters scurry out of the cave. "We can't stay here, it's not safe."

A dusky hue of morning lightened the mouth of the cave as the group watched the entrance for any signs of the creature returning. They were definitely gone…for now.

Brian started untying the rope that bound Carla's feet, then untied her hands as well. He immediately went to work on her foot, ripping her pink pant leg open and tearing off strips. "What's the matter?" she asked them, still laying prostrate on her back.

"Keep your eyes on me Carla," Sadie told her while untying and assessing Dinah's unconscious body. "Can you tell me what happened to Dinah?"

Sadie's eyes were filled with tears as she asked her that, but Carla had no answers to give her. "She's…not who you think she is."

"What do you mean?"

Sadie shook Dinah, slapped her across the cheeks, shouted her name, but she still didn't wake up. All Carla could see was the girls petite chest rising and falling in an obvious rhythm. "I hate to tell you this, but she's a dope-head."

"WHAT?!"

Sadie's shocked face told Carla she had no idea. "I'm sorry," she said, feeling the hurt Sadie was obviously displaying...so much so that she didn't even feel what Brian and Shepherd were doing with her foot anymore.

Sadie flopped her body over top Dinah's chest and sobbed profusely.

Brian noticed how upset she was and finished up with her foot, tying one last knot on Carla's bandaged foot. "Sadie...Pull yourself together," he said. "We need you. Shepherd, help me get Carla up. Pip, you can help Sadie carry Dinah out of here."

The Indian guide seemed distant and detached from the whole situation, but then he'd been like that the whole time out on the boat with her too. He never did say much of anything to her, and they had been together for a week.

"No! the Indian guide suddenly snapped back at Brian, obviously annoyed. "I'll do it myself." He rushed up to Sadie and ordered her to get off Dinah, then he picked the petite blonde up and swung her over his shoulder like a rag-doll. "I owe her!"

The boy eyed Brian as if to tell him not to mess with him. He started for the entrance of the cave.

Sadie sniffled and moved over to Shepherd without saying a word.

"Let's go people," Brian ordered. "We're getting out of here...*now.*"

"Oh no you're not!" a voice answered back from somewhere in the dark part of the cave, steadily moving forward toward the lightened entrance. Leon held his gun on the group, as did Mike and Adam. "You're not going anywhere."

This was Pip's chance. He was the closest to the entrance, he could slip out first before his uncle could notice. But what would happen to the others?

"I didn't think you'd be stupid enough to bring them here Pip?" his uncle scoffed, belittling him like he always did.

"I wouldn't have had to if you would have just left us alone."

"Oh, now what fun would that have been?"

Pip wished he could kill his uncle, be done with him once and for all. He had hurt and killed so many innocent people, he'd be doing the world a favor…But something in his gut told him it wouldn't be right –that vengeance was not his.

"Why don't you let these people go," Shepherd spoke up. "I'm the one you're after. Do whatever you want with me, but let them take the women out of here."

Leon snickered, "You think this is about *you*? You're nobody Shepherd. You hear me, you're *nobody*. You always have been and you always will be."

Mike and Adam laughed this time, holding their guns as if they were *big* men. If the tables were turned, if Pip was the one with the gun, he wondered how tough they would act then.

"You're the *nobody*," Shepherd snapped back.

Leon steadied the gun at Shepherd, narrowing his eyes about to shoot. "Is that right? Come here and say that *loser*."

Right at that moment, something huge, rose from behind Adam, growling with an open jaw above his head, causing Leon to turn. Instead of shooting Shepherd, he aimed for the beast. But it was too late, it's pointy jaws bit off Adam's head, dripping with red frothy blood.

The cave erupted into screams and gunfire.

Carla collapsed to the ground –Sadie and Brian dropped to her side.

Pip had one chance and one chance only, and that was to run with the girl on his back. He might not be able to save anyone else, be he definitely could save Dinah.

So, he did…taking flight like a bird.

Chapter 24

The monster slithered away as the gunfire assaulted it's sleek body, not nearly penetrating it's thick black skin, only grazing it enough to send it away for a while.

Now the four of them faced another demon…the human kind.

"*Let us go Leon*!" Brian shouted, helping Carla to her one good foot. "That thing will come back for us *all*, gun or no gun. You know that don't you?"

"*Python* would never kill me," Ice said. "I am an eagle…I am his brother, something you people would *never* understand."

"Sure looked like he tried to kill you."

"*Shut up*!" Ice shouted, obviously annoyed, "and get away from the entrance."

Leon and Mike used their guns to motion the group to move against the wall. "Let's shoot them," Mike grinned. "We don't need them. We got what we came for, lets just go get Pippi Longstocking and the princess. We don't have much time before the plane gets here anyway."

"Now *you* shut up," Ice turned the gun on Mike.

Mike dropped his gun and held his hands up. "Hey now…just calm down. You don't want to shoot me. I helped you. Who told you which rocks were diamonds? Who told you about meteorite diamonds in the first place? I did *all* the dirty work for you. I made everything happen, *me*, me and…and Carla. Didn't we baby? We made a pretty good team, didn't we?"

He looked at Carla, pleading for help with his sad eyes as Leon held a gun to his head and backed him against a rock.

"I said shut up!"

"*Just wait,*" Mike mumbled pleading for his life. "Carla? You guys? Do something."

For a moment, Brian considered jumping up and defending Mike, but what would *that* do? Leon would just shoot him anyway and then *he'd* be next. No, he'd say a prayer for the guy and the rest would be up to the Lord. Besides, he dropped his gun back there at the entrance where they found the flashlight.

"Baby? I love you honey," Mike cried out, "You have to do something. We could still run away together. I love you. I'm sorry I hurt you. Please...*do something!*"

Suddenly Carla said, "Wait! Don't kill him. He's nothing but slime but he doesn't deserve to die." She looked at Brian and Sadie then. "If *I* can have a second chance then Mike deserves one too."

"Oh baby," Mike cried, "I knew you still loved me."

"I don't Mike, but someone else does and he has a bigger heart than I do."

Leon rolled his eyes, lowering the gun from Mike's head. "Isn't this touching, but I'm afraid it's not up to you *Grandma*," he growled, "it's up to *me.*"

Then Leon booted Mike in the stomach, sending him down on his knees. "He's got a *plane*," Mike rattled on, labouring his speech as he struggled with Leon. "H-he's coming to pick us up this morning...at the north tip of the...*Island.*"

At Mike's last word, Ice fingered the trigger of his gun, aiming it under Mike's chin, blowing the top of his head clear off.

"*No!*" Carla screamed, as a blood shower splattered everywhere.

Luckily Leon hadn't seen Brian crawl near the exit to find his gun or he wouldn't have retrieved it on time. "Hold it right their Leon!"

The two men stood in a standoff, aiming guns at each other.

"What do we have here?" Leon mused. "Checkmate?"

Shepherd picked up Carla and started moving her to the exit. Sadie looked reluctant but followed anyway when Brian motioned her to go.

"Not so fast," Leon said. "Nobody's going anywhere."

"Let the women go."

"Now why would I do that? I'd rather do this. Leon charged at Brian sending him careening to the ground, flipping the gun right out of his hand, landing right in front of Shepherd.

Leon cocked the gun at Brian's head as he lay his wiry body on top of Brian. He didn't even notice where Brian's gun went. "You must be the worst cop I ever saw," he said. "Where'd you get your badge from…a Cracker Jack box?"

Brian saw Shepherd hand Carla over to Sadie out of the corner of his eye, pick up the gun, and head over to them. He grinned and turned back to Leon. "Oh, you're going to wish you never said that."

Leon's smirk turned to a frown the moment Shepherd stuck the gun in the Indian's temple. "You ain't so tough now are you, puke face?" Shepherd mused as he spit. "Drop the gun and get off the cop."

Leon dropped the heavy piece of iron, rose from his position and held his hands up in surrender. Shepherd kicked the gun away. "Now Brian," he said, "get the women out of here."

"No way Shepherd," Brian told him, hoping to knock some sense into the man. *He* was the cop, he was the one with experience, and it would be *him* who would take this prisoner back to where he belonged, not an ex-con.

"*Brian,*" Shepherd ordered, while keeping his eyes focussed on Leon. "I'm not telling you again. Back away, and take those women out of here before I have to do something I'll regret."

"Like what?"

"Like this." Shepherd darted over to where he had kicked Leon's gun, while still aiming at Leon. He knelt to pick it up, aiming one gun at Leon and the other at Brian.

"I hate to do this to you buddy. But you didn't want to listen. Now take those women out of here, or I swear I'll kill you."

Traitor! Brian knew it all along. "Fine!" he said, backing up to Sadie as she laboured with Carla. He took her other arm and helped her hop toward the entrance of the cave, turning around just before leaving.

"Just tell me this Shepherd," Brian struggled with his emotions, "Was Sadie part of the game?"

Sadie broke down and didn't even turn to face the man.

Leon roared with laughter as Shepherd still aimed the gun on him and Brian. "Don't make me shoot you cop," he said. "I don't owe you an explanation. I'm a big boy, I can do what I want without having to ask my *mother.*"

Sadie sobbed loudly this time, but still didn't turn around.

"You're despicable...you know that. How could you do that to her. Sadie doesn't deserve that, she's my friend."

"She's going to be a *dead* friend in a minute if you don't get her out of here."

"Come on ladies lets go, the smell in here is making me sick to my stomach," Brian snapped, wanting to stay and argue, but knowing no matter what he said it wouldn't change a criminal's mind. Once a con always a con.

~~~~

When the three of them were finally out of sight, Shepherd handed Ice the gun. "Who did you think was going to help you carry all these rocks to the plane?" Shepherd grinned at his old prison mate.

"You had me going there for a while, Shep."

"Hey, I surprise myself sometimes."

Shepherd picked up the backpacks from the ground and handed one to Ice and swung the other two over his own shoulders. "If we leave now, we can probably beat the others to the plane. See, I don't like to take hostages. They just slow you down. It's the only way to work man. And if you kill them…that just gets too messy for me. So, calm down bro. I'll get us to the plane…but I want my share of the rocks."

"You got it."

Chapter 25

The bright morning sun was so striking as it pierced through the tall evergreens right into Pip's eyes as he laboured through the bush with Dinah on his back. Every ounce of energy had been spent running as fast as he could away from the cave, and with the beating he received last night, his already weakened body couldn't go on.

As Pip's knees buckled, Dinah slipped off his shoulders and onto the deep moss-covered ground. "*Jesus, I can't do this!*" he cried, panting so hard as he sat beside the palsied girl he should have stood up for last night. It was his fault they took her. It was his fault she ended up like this.

Why did he judge her? Who was *he* to think less of her because of her past? Was he perfect? No, in fact, Dinah reached out to him and shared her faith with him even though she didn't have to. That brought bile to his throat.

He gagged on an empty stomach, moaning in agony. "*Jesus,*" he cried, holding his stomach. "*Forgive me…I hurt my friend. Don't let her die.*"

Bending over her, Pip listened for breathing. It was faint and her breath was warm. *She's still alive.* He opened her eyelids but her pupils were abnormally small.

Pip didn't know that much about drugs, but he watched T.V and learned a lot from the southern stations to know his uncle gave her too much drugs for her petite little body. She probably wasn't even a hundred pounds.

Quickly, he got up and searched around for something his Grandfather told him about. It was a root. A special plant that grew on these northern islands with medicinal purposes. *What was it again?* It looked like a small fern, but it had a blue-green tinge.

He scoured the area, looking under trees and bushes until...There it was. The miniature plant only his Grandfather knew about. He yanked it out of the soil, revealing a thick twisted root that almost looked like a carrot except it had funny blue zebra stripes all over it. *This is it.*

Grandfather had told him his ancestors use to crush it with a rock, smashing the root into a mushy substance, then giving the sick person some of it to eat. But how was he going to make Dinah eat it when she was unconscious?

He'd deal with that when the time came.

With a medium size rock, Pip hammered the root over and over again until there was nothing left. *I'm going to need more than that.* He pulled another plant from the soil and smashed its roots as well, scooping the mush into a mound. *There.*

Now all he had to do was make sure she ate it...but first he had to try and wake her up. "*Dinah!*" he shouted, slapping her face. "*Wake up!*"

She didn't stir.

How could he wake her up? "*Jesus...can you do it?*"

Pip waited for an answer, *something*, but nothing happened. The girl was still unconscious, and neither of them had a lot of time to wait around for her to wake up.

Then he remembered an old fairy tail...Indian style. His grandfather used to tell him this story when he was just a little boy. He used to call it *The Sleeping Warrior* story. It was about a shy scrawny native boy who kissed a sleeping beauty. If she woke up, he turned into a warrior. Why did he think of this story now?

Feeling like a fool, Pip looked to the sky and grinned, "You don't want me to kiss her, do you Jesus? Because that wouldn't be right."

Pip paused for an answer, but no voice told him to do it, he just knew. "Okay Jesus, *if you say so, but don't blame me if nothing happens. I haven't had much practice.*"

Bending over Dinah's soft fair skin, Pip pursed his lips on top of Dinah's pale ones for a little peck, but nothing happened. "*See, I told you Jesus.*"

But something inside of him told him to try again.

This time, Pip pursed his lips to hers again and held his mouth there for a long time, enjoying the soft lengthy kiss. She coughed in response, groaning with her eyes closed. *This is progress.*

Pip grabbed a finger full of root-mush and sat Dinah up. She was still not fully awake, but he would try to make her eat the stuff anyway.

She groaned and made funny faces, but she wasn't waking up. *This is it. Only one shot.* Pip put the mush into her mouth and to the side of her tongue, then he kissed her again until she moved her own mouth around.

She was doing it. When Pip sat back, she groaned and smacked her lips together, sticking her tongue out like a baby trying to eat pabulum for the first time. Her eyes remained closed, but that didn't matter, Pip repeated the procedure until all the root-mush was gone, then he lay her back down in her slumber and waited.

I'll never doubt you again Jesus.

~~~~

" Can someone explain to me what happened back there?"

Nobody wanted to answer her. Sadie and Brian were just dragging her through the bush at an accelerated pace as if they were angry at her or something. Carla knew that wasn't the case, but at least they could stop for a minute and talk to her.

"*Enough*!" she finally shouted. "I can't hop anymore without taking a break."

Brian stopped and bent over to catch his breath while Sadie helped her sit down. They all panted like marathon runners.

"Are you two going to talk to me?"

Brian looked at Sadie, then Sadie hung her head and sobbed. "I-I thought he was a good guy," Sadie cried like a baby. "I thought we could trust him."

"Who? Shepherd?" Carla asked.

"Who do you think Carla?" Brian scolded her, putting an arm around Sadie.

"Oh, come on you guys, Shepherd's one of us. Whatever he's up to, he's doing it for us. Can't you see that?"

"Carla…he's a turncoat," Brian frowned at her. "Believe me, I know one when I see one. I've dealt with these types of people for years. They don't change."

"I changed."

"I know you did," Sadie sniffled, "and we're thankful the Lord spared you. I hope you really meant what you said back there. I hope you really gave your life to the Lord because I'm tired of counterfeit Christians."

"I'm no counterfeit," Carla said, meaning it from the heart. She never thought she'd make it out of the cave alive, leave alone away from those monsters. Just the fact that God spared her at that exact moment she prayed was miracle enough to make her a lifelong believer for real this time.

Why she thought she was a Christian before was beyond her. The feeling she had inside of her now was never there before. It was euphoric…almost as if she was about to explode with joy. This was the Holy Spirit, she knew that much from attending Sunday School and Bible Studies all her life, except, she always used to think people were making their experiences up when they told her they were filled with the Holy Spirit.

Now she new what they were talking about.

"But you know you have to change your life now, don't you Carla?" Sadie sniffled again, almost sounding sceptical. "I *have* changed my life. I will continue to change my life. You'll see. There won't be anymore *Mike'*s in my life anymore. Just my husband…if he'll have me."

But something in Sadie's face told her she didn't believe her. It was understandable after all she had been through. She and Shepherd had developed feelings for each other. To think he's a traitor must hurt. Carla knew that pain all too well. *But Shepherd isn't a traitor.*

She'd prove it, and she'd prove that she wasn't faking her conversion either.

"Come on you guys," Brian interrupted her thoughts. "We have to keep moving. We have a plane to catch, and I want to get there before they do. Now let's move."

"But what about Dinah?" Sadie asked him with sombre eyes.

"Pip has her. I trust him. He'll take care of her. If we run into them, great. But if we don't, we have to go for help without them."

Sadie didn't say anything, she just hung her head.

"Don't worry Sadie," Carla tried to cheer her up, "I'll pray for her."

As the three of them took off through the bush again, Carla prayed like never before, in fact she didn't even feel her aching leg that had plagued her with so much pain up to this point. The Lord was giving her yet another miracle with his own anesthesia.

After they had been going for a while, feeling the exhaustion again, Brian stumbled on some rocks causing the three of them to tumble to the ground.

"Carla...you're foot?" Sadie moaned, sitting up in pain, looking down at her leg.

"What?"

Brian shot his head at Sadie and scooted over to Carla. Blood sopped the entire bandage now. "We have to re-wrap it again," he told her. "Sadie I'm going to need your help."

Carla didn't know what all the fuss was about. Her foot didn't even hurt anymore. It couldn't be that bad...could it?

~~~~

Brian took Sadie aside for a minute and whispered to her. She hadn't really seen the wound with the bandage off, but she figured she could handle it. He didn't need to baby her, especially now.

"What?" she asked right away. "There's nothing else that can shock me."

"This might," Brian whispered.

Sadie rolled her eyes. She was tired, hungry, hot, broken hearted, and annoyed at her friend at this point. "Just spit it out Brian."

"She has no foot."

"*What?*"

"Keep your voice down Sadie. I don't want her to know. We bandaged it up so much that it looks big enough to be a foot. But there *is no foot*. Do you understand what I'm telling you?"

Sadie just nodded. What else could she say.

"I don't know how she's been holding out this long. Most people would have gone into shock by now. The pain alone would knock you right out."

Tears came to Sadie's eyes again. "What do you want to do?"

"The tourniquet I made must have slipped off when we fell. If she loses anymore blood, we'll be carrying her. We have to stop the bleeding and bandage it up with fresh ones. Do you think you could rip off one of your pant legs into strips for me to use as bandages?"

"I guess so, it's 100% cotton." Of course, he didn't know what she meant by that but it didn't matter. All that mattered was Carla. She couldn't lose   her   too.
As they both turned around and headed back to Carla, she started convulsing in front of them.

"*No!*"

Chapter 26

By the time Pip got the idea, he and Dinah we're already in the water when he heard the buzz of the plane. It headed for the northern edge of the island and they were at the south tip –the shortest rout to land.

He figured if he could get Dinah to shore, he could make it to the logging company a few miles inland. It was a risk considering she was still out of it. After she had eaten all the medicine he made for her, she resumed her sleepy state.

Pip swam backwards with his arm supporting Dinah's head while she floated on her back. Just a little longer and he would make it to shore. Only, if he had known about the plane, he might have stayed and tried to overtake it. But at this point he really didn't know who was still alive and who wasn't.

Then, while he kicked his feet, something touched it.

The monster…it's back!

It was circling the two of them.

He swirled his body around back and forth, still holding onto Dinah. *Where is it?* He couldn't see anything in the water at all, but he definitely could feel the nibbling.

"Jesus...help!"

Then, right before the two of them, a large eel-like creature raised its ugly head to the surface, water dripping from its repulsive face. The monster opened it's mouth, bearing a full set of teeth, hissing with its long pointy tongue.

A few feet away, another monster rose from the deep, then a smaller one beside it. *A whole family.* It wasn't exactly warming.

The three of them circled Pip and Dinah as they lay there perfectly still.

Nothing happened.

It was as if the monsters couldn't even see them. They kept circling, acting as if they were trying to find them, but couldn't. They were invisible to them for some reason.

Pip tried not to breathe, he had to move his arms and legs to keep afloat, but without taking deep breaths, he was beginning to sink and so was Dinah.

Jesus...I can't keep this up for long.

Finally, the three creatures slowly moved away, hissing as they left. They dove down below the surface leaving Pip hacking and coughing as he swallowed water.

Regaining his breath, he dragged Dinah the rest of the way to shore, pulling her floppy body into the cold wet sand. He held her then, caressing her head and kissing her cheek. *"We're okay Dinah...We're going to be okay."*

~~~

The convulsions stopped and so did the bleeding, but Brian didn't know for how long. It was touch and go with Carla. She lost a lot of blood, and had a weak pulse. If he didn't get help soon, she wasn't going to make it.

A bush plane flew low overhead as Brian and Sadie knelt beside Carla praying. Brian could tell the plane was getting ready to land. "We better go," he said. "I'll carry her on my back. We can't be that far from shore."

Sadie said nothing. He could tell she was just as tired as he was. Things didn't look good at this point. Brian wondered what would happen to the women when he got to the plane. Would Leon and Shepherd already be there? Is he just leading these two women to their deaths? It was all hopeless.

Brian thought of his wife and sons. Would he ever see them again? If this was it, if this was the end of his life, it had been a good one. He had been loved by the best, and blessed with sons that loved and adored him. He had nothing to complain about.

As they approached the rocky beach, Brian drew back when he heard voices. It was Leon and Shepherd. *Great.* They *did* make it ahead of them. Of course, they weren't hauling an injured woman on their back.

Brian set Carla down, propping her up against a boulder. "I've got to get a little closer Sadie. You stay here with Carla."

"No! I'm going with you."

Why did she have to be obstinate *now*? "Look Sadie," he sighed, putting both hands on her shoulders. "I just want to get closer so I can listen to what they're saying. I'm not leaving you here. I'll be right back...Okay?"

"You better."

"I promise."

Slowly Brian crept rock to rock, staying low enough without being seen, but close enough to hear what they were saying.

The guy in the plane finally came out, tip toeing over a few rocks until he met up with Leon and Shepherd. "You guys ready?" he said.

"Not quite, we could only get our backpacks up to that ridge. We just need to go get them, and we'll be on our way," Leon told him. Shepherd didn't say anything, he just went along with him like a fool.

"Thanks again for doing this bud," Leon told the pilot. "You don't know how much this means."

"No pro-blem-o," the pilot smiled, shaking Leon's hand. "I told you I owe ya one, and I meant it. As far as I'm concerned. I still owe ya. This here guy pretty well saved my life in the joint. If it wasn't for him, I'd still be doing time."

"No kiddin'," Shepherd smiled, shaking the guys hand. "Must have been in Vancouver because I never saw you in the Pen before."

This conversation was making Brian sick.

Shepherd went on talking to the pilot. He jigged up and down as if he was cold, and looked around nervously. *Well he should be nervous.* He had a lot to be nervous about. When Brian got his hands on him, he'd be sorry he ever met him.

"Come on Shepherd," Leon complained, "Are you Chatty Cathy or something?"

"Hey! I can talk can't I."

"Do it on your own time pal," Leon grumbled, "or you don't get your cut."

"Fine," Shepherd sighed, shaking the pilots hand for the second time, looking around nervously again. "I guess we'll talk later man."

Brian ducked behind the rock, afraid Shepherd almost saw him. Sadie's head was so high over the rock back there he was afraid he saw her for sure. *Great, and this was a perfect opportunity to take the plane.* All he had to do was knock out the pilot…but what about Sadie with her head flying as high as a kite? He'd have to go back and get her, or she could spoil everything.

Or…

Brian waved Sadie over to him. He stood for a split second making sure the pilot didn't see him, and Leon and Shepherd had their backs to him. He motioned for her to come and then he picked up a rock to hit the pilot over the head.

Okay…calm down Brian. You can do this.

With full force, Brian stood and thwacked the pilot over the head. His body immediately collapsed to the gravel. *That was easy.*

Sadie rushed up to him, ducking as she approached. "Good job Brian!"

"Help me get him into the plane and tie him up, hurry, before they see us."

The two of them got him into the plane and hurried as they wrapped a rope around his hands and feet, gagging him with a small white rag. "Roll him under the seats back there."

Brian kept poking his head out of the window to check on Leon and Shepherd. They were still up on the cliff. *Good.* "Sadie, I'm going to go get Carla," he told her. "I think I still have time. I want you to hide in the back of the plane and don't come out until you hear my voice. Do you hear me?"

"Loud and clear."

Brian rushed off to get Carla, eyed Leon and Shepherd coming down the hill, swung Carla over his shoulder, and started to run.

Lord almighty…let this work.

~~~

He was taking too long.

Sadie already heard voices and she didn't recognize Brian's. Leon and Shepherd were back, but where was Brian? Should she come out of the tarp she was hiding under?

Something told her not too. Instead she just listened.

"We beat you to it cop," Leon said plainly as he stood outside the plane.

"Where's Sadie?" Shepherd asked Brian.

"What do you care."

Sadie felt her heart sink. It was all she could do to stay under the tarp.

"Where's the pilot, that's what *I* want to know?" Leon said.

"He went for a swim, where do you think."

"Ah, I didn't know a cop could be so clever," Leon toyed with him, "But you're not as smart as you think you are. I can fly this bird too you know...now drop the broad and get in."

"She's sick."

"I don't care," Leon snapped. "Shoot her, Shep."

"No! She's going with us," Shepherd said surprising Sadie. "I at least want one broad out of this deal. You know how long it's been. She's no good to me dead."

You sick pervert...and to think I liked you.

"Oh *fine*," Leon spit, "put her in the back then."

Shepherd approached the back where Sadie was hiding. *He's going to see me, he's going to see the pilot too.* Then, as Shepherd lowered his head, bending forward to lay Carla down on the floor of the plane, she saw him looking at the pilot's body.

Sadie couldn't help it, she gasped in a panic.

I'm dead, I'm dead.

Out of the corner of the tarp, Sadie met Shepherd's eyes. They locked in that moment, frozen in time far away from this one. She wanted to say something, wanted to tell him to leave her alone. Her eyes were so wide and dry she was afraid to blink.

Then...just when she saw him about to tell on her, he did something so unpredictable even *she* didn't expect it.

He held his finger over his pursed mouth, shushing her as he gave her a wink.

Chapter 27

Leon sat down in the pilot's seat and turned the key sputtering the big bush plane's propeller to life. It reminded Brian of the last time he flew a big beast like this –five years ago.

Shepherd had the gun to his head as he sat in the jump seat of the plane. If it wasn't for that fool, he could have at least tried to tackle Leon, but it was hopeless now, the plane was about to take off. Once they were in the air, it would be too risky. *Thanks a lot Shepherd.*

The plane started gaining speed, bouncing over the choppy water. Leon flicked all the right button's and turned to Shepherd just before taking off. *This is it.* Brian could take a swing at Leon while he had his head turned and he could gain control of the plane, but what about Shepherd, he'd shoot him in an instant.

The two men continued to talk about plane instruments, while Brian sat there contemplating his next move. He was willing to risk anything at this point.

Brian socked Leon square in the jaw, elbowing Shepherd behind him. The plane slowed and veered to the right, knocking Leon's gun to the floor of the plane. Shepherd still held his but buckled from the elbow in the ribs he gave him.

Brian picked up the gun.

The plane headed for the cliff.

"Drop the gun Shepherd," Brian panted jabbing his own weapon into Leon's temple, "Or I swear I'll shoot him."

Shepherd raised booth hands, still holding the gun. *"We're going to hit the cliff you dummy."*

Brian turned around, leaning into the cockpit, steering the plane to safety and switching off all the necessary buttons while still holding the gun on Leon. "Not anymore were not, now hand me the gun Shepherd, or I swear I'll shoot you both."

"You can fly?" Shepherd asked Brian with wide eyes.

"What? Of course, I can."

Then, just as Brian turned his head slightly, Leon elbowed the side of his face, knocking him into the seats. The gun flew out of his hands, landing on the floor, sliding away from them.

Leon laughed, "*Checkmate*. It seems we're one up on you again cop, and this time we're not going to be so soft. Shepherd you were right, taking hostages just slows us down…so shoot the idiot will you pal. I've had enough of him already."

Brian looked to Shepherd while he still aimed the gun on him, then Shepherd turned to Leon…*gun and all*. "Sorry Ice, I got to take care of my *people*. Hands up where I can see them."

"You dirty…" Leon growled, cussing every swear word under the sun. "I knew I couldn't trust you. You conned me."

"You bet I did."

Brian couldn't believe it. He didn't know what to think, or feel. He methodically got up off the seats and retrieved the gun. *Boy was he wrong about Shepherd. Leopards could apparently change their spots after all.*

"I-I don't know what to say," Brian stuttered, standing beside Shepherd with both guns now aimed at Leon.

"Don't say anything. I did what I had to do."

But you didn't have to.

The two men tied Leon's feet and hands and sat him down in a seat somewhere in the middle. Shepherd took the seat next to him and aimed the gun at him just in case he tried anything.

"Let's get out of here Brian," Shepherd grinned. "You know, I wish you would have told me you could fly. I would have kicked Ice's butt a whole lot sooner. Man...here I was thinking he was the only pilot we had."

"How was I supposed to tell you I could fly?" Brian mused, settling himself down in the pilots seat, flicking the switches on the instrument panels, roaring the bird to life again. "Was I supposed to stand up and flap my arms like wings?"

The two of them laughed at each other.

"It's good to have you back on our side again Shepherd, Isn't it Sadie?" Heads turned to the back of the plane. "You can come out now Sadie...It's safe."

Sadie lifted the tarp, crouching as she revealed her teary face. She met Shepherd's eyes and he met hers.

"Oh, how touching," Leon balked.

"*Shut up!*" Brian interrupted. "You don't *get* to talk."

Brian turned back to his instruments and focused on getting them out of there. He listened to the conversation going on behind him and smirked.

"I'm going to check on Carla and the Pilot and then I'm going to come up there and talk to you, you little brat."

"Lookin' forward to it babe. I hope you're not gonna beat me up though," Shepherd giggled. "I was worried that you wouldn't forgive me. I thought you'd hate me forever."

"Oh, don't worry about that," she answered back. "You had me at the wink."

Wink?

Brian shook his head and laughed out loud. He was glad Sadie still had a sense of humour. She was quite the character. She had a personality like Jenny, and that made him smile all the more. He could hardly wait to see his wife again.

As Brian increased speed, preparing to take off, he scoured the edges of the island for Pip and Dinah, the group wasn't complete until he found those two, but he knew he had to leave if he didn't see them soon. Carla needed immediate medical attention, and the pilot did too.

He said a prayer for his lost friend and the girl he carried on his back, and prepared for take-off.

Then –*bang*, the plane thumped, hitting something with one of its pontoons.

"*What was that?*" Sadie cried.

"I don't know!" Brian checked his instruments – nothing out of the ordinary. He checked the water – no rocks. Then, as the plane suddenly slowed to a crawl without him doing it, he realized something was terribly wrong.

"Everyone stay where you are." The plane teetered side to side like a rocky boat. Something had a hold of the pontoon and was pulling them backward.

Sadie screamed while Shepherd and Brian jumped out of their seats and looked out the window. Behind the tip of the plane's tail, a large black shiny head rose above the water. *"My Lord,"* Brian cried, *"It's back!"*

"What do we do?" Sadie panicked, holding tightly to the seats as the plane rocked wildly side to side.

Leon just sat there with a smile on his face, closing his eyes as if he were praying.

"The engine's still running," Shepherd shouted, "see if you can still take off."

Then, the giant sea serpent rose to its glory, hissing and batting the plane around with its large head as if it were a tiny toy plane.

Shepherd opened the door, hanging his body out of the plane. "What are you doing," Brian called to him. "*Get back inside.*"

Then the shooting started. Shepherd peppered the large creature with his gun until it drew back from them. "Okay Brian," he shouted, "hit it."

Brian tried to accelerate, but the plane laboured. Something was still holding it back. "I can't!" he shouted out the door to Shepherd, who was now completely outside, tiptoeing over the pontoons.

Lord in heaven...what is that man doing now?

~~~

If he could only get to the back, there was something hanging on the tip of the right pontoon. But he'd have to be careful because that thing was coming straight for him again. *Walk by faith not by sight.*

Shepherd glanced into the last window of the plane as he stepped by. Sadie's face was pasted to it, eyes as big and saucers. *Don't look at her, don't look at her. Just keep going and you'll be fine.*

When he got to the end of the pontoon, he realized what it was that was holding them up, it was a smaller creature just like the big one...but it was obviously dead, tangled around the pontoon. That was probably what they hit.

Shepherd bent down to remove the thing, kicked at it's miniature head, and watched it sink below the water. The adult was right in front of him when he finished, roaring now, ready to attack.

Shepherd aimed his gun, took a few pock shots at him, and then ran out of ammo. *Rats!* He dropped the gun and quickly stepped toward the door, but just before he got there, another mid-sized creature reared its ugly head, snapping at him with its sharp teeth. *"Go!"* he shouted to Brian as he stood there in the doorway.

"Get in!"

The plane rolled ahead, gaining speed now, leaving the two creatures lagging behind, but Shepherd couldn't seem to make it in the door yet. The wind was too strong.

"I can't make it! Just take off."

Wind flipped Shepherd's hair as he held on for dear life, trying to force himself upward into the small doorway. Then as the plane slowly rose off the water, Shepherd felt someone's hand touching his. He looked up to find a gun barrel to his face.

Rats! Shepherd jeered to the left as a bullet whizzed past him. It was Ice, he must have cut his ropes off and grabbed the other gun. Another shot whizzed by, causing him to lose his balance, nearly falling off the pontoon.

As the plane began to climb, Shepherd noticed the creatures were still following them...and Ice was now outside of the plane like he was, ready for a chase. *"Give it up, Shep!"* the wild man shouted. *"I win!* I'm gonna shoot you dead and then take this plane straight to hell."

"Not if I can help it."

"What are *you* going to do about it?" Ice laughed aiming the gun at him.

Before he knew what happened, Ice shot him straight through the shoulder, causing him to dangle from the wing of the plane with only one arm.

"Say bye-bye, *loser*!" Ice smiled just as the plane veered right, knocking him around a little. Shepherd held on for dear life just to watch the man regain his firm grip on the door.

Then, like an angel sent from God, Sadie reached out the door and thwacked the man over the head with a fish cleaning board. *All right!*

Ice dropped the gun, lost his balance and fell from the doorway to the pontoon below. *Now who's the loser.* He dangled their exposed to the demons below.

Shepherd just stood their, both feet firmly planted on the pontoon, one hand gripping the wing of the plane. "You're finished Ice!"

Ice glanced below to the blue water beneath him, dangling there like bait as the largest creature thrust itself out of the surface of the deep –biting off the man's entire lower extremities from the waist down.

Blood spewed everywhere as the creature took his portion down to the water.

Shepherd stayed where he was, stunned at what just happened. He swallowed hard, wind whipping his face as he looked at the half body of the man still hanging there.

"I-I'll see you in hell," the wincing man stuttered, releasing his fingers as the top half of his body plummeted to the creatures below.

I've already been there!

"Grab the rope," he heard a voice shouting as he turned his eyes away from the mayhem. It was the angel again, reaching with her wings to bring him up to heaven.

"Snap out of it and try to reach it."

What?

Was his mind playing tricks on him, or was the dizziness he was feeling making him imagine an angel was standing next to him. Now she's tying a rope around his waist.

"Move your feet!" the angel shouted to him, inching him closer and closer to the door. He wasn't sure what he was grabbing on to, just that her wings made it seem like they were floating.

I love you angel.

Suddenly, he felt his body warm from the cold wind that use to be hitting his face. He was inside the plane now, but someone was slapping him, slapping him *hard*.

"Are you okay?"

Chapter 28

Pip was tired, his feet were barely moving now. Dinah's petite body that once felt so light on his back, now felt like a brick house. One more step and he would drop.

He had been following the beach westward now for miles. He couldn't even see Reefers island anymore. All he could see was that storm coming in from the North.

I surrender.

Without warning, Pip dropped to the sand as Dinah's lethargic body rolled off his shoulders. His mouth was dry, cracked with blood, and his head still throbbed from the beating he received from the night before.

Dinah lay there still and undisturbed. She had been spared the trauma the day had bestowed upon them all. But Pip wondered what other kind of trauma she may have sustained. His root-mush didn't give him any signs of hope that it was working at all.

"Jesus…" he crouched down before the petite blonde. She looked so helpless, so young. *"I can't go on,"* he sobbed, feeling his ribs crushing as his chest shook up and down. *"I don't have any strength left to give."*

As the noisy waves rushed in succession upon the wet sandy beach, Pip bent over to kiss Dinah for the last time. He lay his body next to hers and wept severely. *"I have nothing left to give, Jesus. I'm sorry. I failed you…I failed her. I don't want to live anymore. Take my life and give it to her."*

Pip lay there, wiping his streaming tears. If Dinah died, he would be the only one left. Nobody knew where he was, and probably nobody survived Reefers Island either.

Then something occurred to him. Why should he wait around for a wolf or something to rip him apart? How could he? He'd seen animal attacks before, and he definitely didn't want to end up like that.

He looked around for anything sharp, a piece of metal, glass, something. Then he found the perfect weapon. It was sharp enough. The twig was strong and pointy and would serve him well.

It shouldn't be too hard to drive it straight through his own heart, it already broke into millions of tiny pieces the moment he pushed Dinah away last night. *How could he.* Just looking at her sweet cherub face brought back the heartbreaking memory. He couldn't imagine a greater pain than that.

Yes, he would do it. He would end his own life…and maybe *just maybe* Jesus would give it to *her*.

~~~

As the thunder clashed against the plane, and the sky grew dark against the horizon, the tattered bush plane meandered through the air against all odds. It wasn't just fate that got them off the island and away from evil. It wasn't good luck, it was her Savior that did it. Sadie knew that for sure.

Now, after she checked on the three patients, she went to talk to Brian up front. "He'll be alright," she said. "He lost a lot of blood from the bullet wound but I compressed it as much as possible."

"And Carla?"

"I don't know. But the pilot is starting to wake up. That's good news. You didn't kill him after all."

"Great, just make sure he doesn't cause any trouble."

Sadie knew he wouldn't. She made double sure by tying his arms behind his back and attaching them to the frame of the seat. There was no way he was getting free like Leon did.

"Do you think we'll beat the storm?" she asked Brian as he punched another button on the instrument panel.

"We better, we got a long flight ahead of us and we don't need any more trouble."

"I can't help but think about Dinah. Do you think she's okay?"

Brian didn't answer her, he pretended he had to fidget with a gauge. That was just his way of avoiding the topic but she could tell it bothered him too. "I've prayed a hundred times for Dinah but then God doesn't always do what *we* want does he. Look what happened to…"

Brian interrupted her, obviously annoyed. "Not another word about Dinah, please."

"But…"

"Why don't you go back there and check on the others again."

Denial was an interesting part of grief. It made times like this tolerable. *Fine.* Maybe she could get some rest too, she had been running on adrenaline for the last two days. It was time to rest.

As she peered over at the patients making sure there was no change, she chose a seat beside a window, looking down at the water below. They weren't high enough to be in the clouds above them, but that was okay with her. She could take in the beauty that God had made.

Sadie didn't realize until now how beautiful this place was. She hadn't been on a plane in a while, and nothing compared to it. Everything looked like a painting from this vantage point, especially the winding twisting beach that edged the lake. It was...

"Brian!" she jumped. "I see something down there on the beach. Two people laying on the sand. Do you see them?"

"No!"

"It's Dinah...I just *know* it."

Brian wasn't answering her. He wasn't getting excited either. How could he ignore her at a time like this? "Brian! Do you see them?"

She could hear Brian sighing. "Are you *sure* you see something?"

"Of course, I'm sure, *now take the plane down!*"

As Brian circled the area making an approach to land, Sadie's heart almost skipped a beat. *Finally,* they had found Dinah. She was going to be okay. Her butterfly had not been taken from her after all.

Thank you, Lord!

Chapter 29

Two weeks later

The rain drizzled down on the small group as they stood beside the two graves as the preacher spoke a few quick words to get them out of the rain. Not many came for the funeral, just Sadie, Shepherd, Carla, Brian, and Jenny.

It was a better place for them to rest. The weather in Prince Albert was about the same, but the cemetery beside Brian's little church was much more personal…and proper for them both.

A sombre mood drifted over the group as they said their final goodbyes. Sadie didn't think she had any more tears to shed, but the hot steamy ones that now meandered down her cold cheeks surprised her. If only she could have done things differently, they might still be alive today.

Shepherd hugged her with his good arm that was still bandaged from the gunshot wound, while she held the dripping wet umbrella over the two of them. "There was nothing you could do," he told her trying to comfort her.

Even though she knew he was right, she still couldn't help but feel responsible.

Brian and Jenny held hands in their long trench coats, shivering under their umbrella. Sadie was glad Brian came out of this unscathed. Jenny had her husband back…a little shaken…but back just the same.

God was a good God seeing them through, but he also used the situation to change people. Her life would never be the same. She had found something she never thought she'd ever get to experience – Love. It wasn't supposed to happen to an old spinster like her, but it did. Now she and Shepherd had all the time in the world to get to know each other, and it was something to look forward to.

"They made it," Carla turned, twisting with her crutches, alerting everyone.

Sadie's heart pounded as she spun around, almost slipping in the rain. It was hard to focus on them at first, the day was so grey, but there they were…walking hand in hand.

A true-blue miracle.

"We thought you'd never get here," Carla beamed.

Brian smiled, "Glad you could make it. It wouldn't be the same without you two."

Sadie immediately went over to hug the two of them, afraid to ever let her little butterfly out of her sight again. But this time she knew she had to. It was time for her to grow up, to spread her wings and fly.

From the moment they rescued Dinah on the beach that day, Sadie knew she was going to make it. And after spending two weeks in the hospital, she proved that she was a fighter.

And Pip…the young man that had saved her life. Sadie would be forever grateful. When she found out he was about to end his own life on the beach that day…and didn't, all she could say was *Praise the Lord.*

It was God who stopped him, he explained to them all later. He told them how Dinah had helped him find Jesus and bring them to the beach that day to save their lives. *A miracle* he told them, and it was a miracle Dinah even survived.

The doctors told her most people never survive overdoses, but they found traces of a foreign substance in her bloodstream that counteracted the drug. When Sadie asked Pip about it, all he did was smile.

"Well, we better get going," Dinah told the group. "I just wanted to stop by and pay my respects to Eunice and her baby before my plane leaves."

"What?" Sadie frowned. "Where are you going? You just got out of the hospital."

Dinah looked at Pip, then to her. "I'm going back to rehab today. I need to."

Sadie's eyes filled with tears. "But they're expecting you at the group home next week. I arranged everything."

"I can't go Sadie. After I've spent a few months in rehab, I'll come back. But I'm coming back to Shining Star. It's my home...*you're* my home Sadie."

Sadie didn't know what to say. Her heart pounded and she didn't have breath to speak. All she could do was hug the girl she had spent so much time and effort with, the girl that had quickly become...a *real* daughter to her.

"This decision doesn't have anything to do with a certain native boy, does it?" Brian teased, elbowing Pip in the side.

Pip blushed, smiling like a Cheshire cat.

Dinah turned to Pip with a bashful grin, "As a matter of fact it does."

Chapter 30

Carla wanted to cry but she had already done too much of that. After recovering in the hospital right along side Dinah, she knew ahead of time what the young teenage couple had planned, and was forced to keep it quiet. And now, after seeing the two of them together, she recognized that kind of love.

She thought she was in love with Mike, but that wasn't real. She let her life get so contaminated with sin, she couldn't even notice how toxic it really was until taking that trip to Deep Bay.

It opened her eyes…God opened her eyes.

Her new commitment to the Lord was real…that much she knew. Some might not think so, but she knew –even if it took a lifetime to prove.

The relic of her old self was gone forever, buried beneath a mound of pain…but not forgotten. How could she forget? It was such an integral part of who she was that forgetting about her roots would change her completely.

Sadie didn't agree with her. She told her to give God her past –to just let it go as if it never happened. How could she do that?

"Let God heal you," Sadie told her repeatedly.

But little did the bush woman know that she had already been healed. Even though she lost most of her right leg, she still felt whole and she didn't need a sceptic like Sadie to doubt her.

No…all she needed was someone to believe in her…to respect her.

"Are you ready to go babe?" a handsome voice whispered in her ear, approaching her from behind while she waited under a tree at the cemetery gate.

It was Rod, the handsome surgeon who worked on her leg. "I'm ready if you are," she said kissing him as she got into his BMW, rain sprinkling the windshield.

As the two of them sped off into the mist, Carla wrapped her arms around her new-found love and whispered in his ear. "I love you honey. I'm so excited to be moving in with you."

And even though her stomach ached and told her not to proceed, to turn around and run...she chose to do the opposite, telling herself it would be different this time...realizing she was right all along.

She couldn't forget...the *relic*.

I hope that you enjoyed the story Deep Bay *Relic* and understand that we as Christian's must choose to turn from our sinful ways. In turning from our sin, we leave the past behind us so that we can live a brand-new life. Unlike Carla who in the end chose to go back to her sinful lifestyle, we as Christian's must fight the urge to idolize the past so we don't bring back...*the relic*.

If you haven't read the first book in the Deep Bay series please download it at the Amazon.com

Book Three, *Deep Bay Legacy,* is the next book in the series. Here is a sample of the last book in the series.

DEEP BAY LEGACY - Chapter 1

The waiting room was hot and sticky.

Pip couldn't believe how humid it was for the beginning of June, and the stifling heat made Dinah's pregnancy uncomfortable. Her contractions started by noon yesterday, and gradually got worse throughout the day. By suppertime, he took her to the hospital.

The doctor let Dinah go overdo two weeks, and that annoyed Pip. He was told that wasn't safe. In fact, he was told they would induce after ten days overdue, but it didn't happen. That made him wonder what kind of quack would let her go so long. It was probably why she was having problems.

If something happens to her, or the baby, that doctor will be the one to pay.

Pip wrung his hands as he slumped in a hard orange chair in the waiting room. Every fearful thought ran through his mind. Heart pounding, mouth dry, he could barely breathe as he waited impatiently. Why would they kick him out?

He put his green scrubs on like they told him to, and was prepared for the C-section, but they kicked him out. He understood why she needed surgery, especially with the baby in distress, but why couldn't he be there? She was *his* wife.

Pip bit his nails nervously. No one else was in the waiting room, luckily. Tears streamed down his cheeks, embarrassing for a 25-year-old man. Yet, it was a hospital, and emotional upset was common place, but not for him.

He kept going over details. One minute the monitors were fine, the next they started beeping.

Doctors and residents hurried in, nurses bumped into equipment as they rushed around to see what was going on. "The baby's heart rate just took a nose dive!" That's when the doctor ordered him out like he was nobody important. "I'm sorry, Mr. Eaglefeather, we're going to have to ask you to step outside and let us do our work. We need to get the baby out as fast as possible."

At that point, Pip started to feel the bile rising in his throat. How could God bring him this far, and then let everything fall apart? What was going to happen to his wife and baby? Would they be okay, or would he lose everything like when he was a boy? He escaped a childhood of trauma growing up in northern Saskatchewan, witnessing murders, and almost losing his life a few times, living in the bush with his grandfather.

Then, when he met Dinah and found out what kind of childhood she came from, growing up in foster homes, messed up on drugs, getting caught up with the wrong crowd, it was no wonder he found her at the healing lodge.

It was called *Shining Star Lodge*, run by a nice old lady named, Sadie. She helped Dinah become the woman she is today, the future mother of his child. Surely God won't let anything bad happen to them.

Surely!

Pip's stomach grumbled, yet he knew he couldn't eat anything or it would go straight through him as it had done all through the night. His legs were getting cramped, so he decided he'd stretch them and pace the floors again. What else could he do at this point?

Walking toward the window, Pip looked out at the rain, wondering where it had been for so many weeks. Why the long dry spell? Why such heat? Why couldn't the rain have come two weeks ago when Dinah was crying her eyes out with swollen ankles, sweating in their non-air-conditioned apartment? It was the first on his to-do list: Find them a home to live in, instead of a grungy stifling apartment.

They lived there for the first three years of their marriage, and Pip had enough. It was hard to find good accommodations in Saskatoon, and that's where his job was, so moving out of the city wasn't an option. Sure, he wanted to, but he didn't know how. The thought of raising a child in the big city scared him, especially where they lived. The west side was slowly becoming the slums. Homeless people were usually found outside their apartment building, and petty thefts and assaults happened all the time.

God, help me get my family out of here, he prayed, choking back tears. He leaned against the cold damp window, as streams of rain trickled down, and continued to pray in earnest. He prayed for the safety of his wife. He prayed for the safety of his unborn child, and he prayed for the situation to end in a positive way.

Sniffling, Pip realized he should have called people. Having someone to sit with in the waiting room would have been nice, but he couldn't exactly call them now, especially his family. He hadn't heard from them in years. They went their own way after the Deep Bay incident, during his childhood.

After his uncle's death, and the tragic death of one of his older brothers, his middle brother moved to Prince Albert and was usually in and out of the P.A Pen for some drug trafficking violation or another. He didn't want any part of that lifestyle, nor did his brother want anything to do with a *Bible thumper*, he called him. And Grandfather, and Grayling were both dead now. Pip had felt alone for quite some time, but what could he do about it? He didn't have family like everyone else, except maybe co-workers and Facebook friends, and that wasn't the same.

Since Dinah had no family and he had no family, it made him want children all the more. And sure, he kept in touch with those that helped him through his difficult teenage years and the trauma both he and Dinah sustained at Deep Bay, but they had their own lives to live. He promised to call Loretta and Ben as soon as the baby was born, but the baby wasn't born yet, and they were miles away. They had their own grandchildren. And Brian and his wife had moved half across the country. They kept in touch from time to time, usually at Christmas, but that was it.

Since moving to Saskatoon four years ago, he lost touch with most of his friends and acquaintances. He got used to it after a while. Sadie, the old lady who helped Dinah recover as a teenager at *Shining Star Lodge,* is still running the place out there, and gives them a call occasionally, but she's too far away to do any good at all.

"Find a church," Sadie told him. "You need fellowship." But both he and Dinah tried several churches and didn't feel comfortable at any of them. It was just too hard to fit in, especially with him being aboriginal and Dinah being a white woman. They felt like outsiders most of the time.

They just stayed home on Sunday mornings and had their own little Bible study, and sang their own worship songs. Mostly they were just too tired to go anywhere, anyway. After a week of work, including

Saturday's, Sunday was really the only day off they had together. It was a shame really. It seemed like the world was getting way too busy for its own good.

Pip's job at Mainway Hardware didn't pay very much but it was all he could get when he first moved to Saskatoon. And without any training or money saved to go to school, it was the best he could get. Sure he moved up the ladder, and was now supervisor in the paint department, but still it didn't pay well. And with a new baby coming, he already started to apply for different jobs. Nobody was hiring. *And while I'm asking, God,* he prayed again, *I need a new job. I need something that's going to pay the bills so Dinah doesn't have to go back to work. And I need a new place for my family so they feel safe.*

Pip brushed away another tear, noticing the rain was really coming down now. The farmers wouldn't be happy, but he was. He loved rain. It rained a lot in northern Saskatchewan where he was from. He missed that very much.

At times, mostly during rush-hour traffic, he longed to go back home to Deep Bay. One time he and Dinah almost moved back there, but it wasn't meant to be. Plans fell through, money ran out, and they had to make a living somehow. Dinah took a job as a librarian at Plainsview Elementary School for a few hours a day. It didn't pay well but it supported her passion; and her passion was writing. She was working on her first book.

In the evening, she worked at the Steakhouse as a waitress. Her tips were good, but Pip advised her to quit when she kept coming home exhausted and swollen every night. She was already six months pregnant and needed to get off her feet. Their income took a nosedive, but he didn't care. His wife and baby were more important.

"Why don't you go to school, Pip?" Sadie always told him whenever she phoned from the Shining Star Lodge. "There's government funding for you. I can send you a list of Aboriginal scholarship programs you can apply for." But he always said no. His excuse was that he didn't want to take a handout, and he felt like that's what it was. He didn't want to fall into the same category as most of the aboriginal students out there, and the assumption that their education was somehow cheapened because it was paid for by the government.

It was bad enough that he had a stigma attached to him, and the only thing people saw was the color of his skin. No, he would not take any government handout. He would make his own way. It was something both grandfather and Grayling drilled into him at a young age. Grandfather used to always say, "We may not have much, and there isn't a lot I can give you, but there is one thing: Dignity, Pipata Eaglefeather. Be proud of who you are and where you came from, and carve your own path as your ancestors did."

And so he had. Life was about making choices, and he knew that when he chose not to go to school. But now, there was a new reason to make a better life. His baby was about to be born and that changed everything. At least he could find a better job, even if he didn't go to school. There was always something out there. Trusting God was what he had done in the past and planned to do for the future. He just needed to get through this.

Pip gave his head a shake. Why was this stuff on his mind right now, anyway? He was too tired to think straight. He raked his shaky fingers through his hair and sat back down on the orange chair. Surely, it wouldn't take much longer for the doctor to let him know what was going on. The not knowing, was killing him.

~~~~

Sadie leafed through her address book looking for Pip's cell phone number. She hadn't heard from him in over a week and the baby was due two weeks ago. She wondered if he had forgotten to call. But surely he wouldn't have forgotten something as important as that. Still, she worried about the two of them. They were not doing very well. If only they would find a church of their own to worship in, they would have the fellowship they needed.

Loneliness was something Sadie knew a great deal about. She wished there was someone else besides her, living at Shining Star Lodge. Sure the guests came and went, but that wasn't the same. She needed companionship as much as Pip and Dinah did.

For the longest time she had been trying to find a way for the board to hire a second maintenance worker. The regular guy wasn't very reliable and when he did show up, he usually didn't do a very good job. It was hard to find reliable workers in the north, and that was exactly her point for hiring a second maintenance worker.

The last time a job was available at Shining Star Lodge, Pip almost moved back, but by the time he decided to take it, the board had already hired someone else: The current lazy maintenance man, Abdul. A decision Sadie wished she could overturn. But perhaps a request for a second full time maintenance man would be approved soon, and she could get Pip and Dinah and their new baby out permanently. Dinah could write all she wanted then. Her little butterfly. Oh how she missed her over the years. It was time to come back home.

But then maybe it wasn't home for them? They were both young, and sometimes when you're young, you want to be as far away from home as possible. Pip especially, he left a lot of pain behind when he moved down south. It wasn't likely he'd want to come back to that. He didn't even have any relatives in the area anymore. The only one he did have, was in prison.

Sadie shook her head and continued to leaf through the address book. Normally she would know the number off the top of her head, but lately she was forgetting things. Perhaps she could chalk it down to old age, but that wasn't the only reason. Mostly she was just unorganized, and running the lodge by herself was a great undertaking. So much so, that it was overwhelming most days.

No, she didn't just need a second maintenance man, she needed a kitchen helper, someone to do the boat work, and housekeeping staff. Trying to do it all on her own was only making her look older, faster. Already her mouse-grey hair was quickly turning white. No man would ever want her now. Sure, when the incident at Shining Star Lodge happened years back, she met a man that took an interest in her. But he was only passing through, and didn't want to stay in such an isolated area, as much as he professed he cared for her.

It wasn't meant to be. No, if God wanted her to find love, He would have to find her someone that would make his home at the lodge with her. Until then, she would have to settle for the many guests that would come and go each month.

It sure would be nice to have familiar faces around, and a baby to dote over. Bring back my butterfly to me! she prayed aloud, then paused, hoping for an audible answer. But God usually wasn't as direct as that. No, she knew the way it worked. Experience told her that God's answers were never, no, but rather, not now, or, I have something else in mind.

When people say God doesn't answer prayers, or He says no all the time, she knew differently. She knew it was only a matter of time before something would happen. And what that something was, was always a big surprise. Still, Sadie hoped the surprise was what she wanted.

There it is, she smiled, running her finger down the last page of the address book. What was Eaglefeather doing under, Z? It was a mystery to her, but at least she found the number. She'd give him a call right away.

~~~

"Pip? Is that you?"

"Yeah, it's me."

"Why so down my boy?"

Pip didn't want to explain the situation, but he figured he owed it to her. Sadie was their closest friend, and the more people praying for Dinah and the baby, the better. It was just hard to rehash everything, so he figured he'd give her the short form. "Dinah is having emergency surgery."

"What? Right now? Is everything okay?"

"I don't know." Pip fought back the tears. He didn't know if saying it aloud was what started the emotional roller coaster, or hearing a familiar voice that made him break down. But whatever the reason, it was a long time coming.

"Is it the baby?"

"Yes!" He continued to sob. "Dinah was in labor, and then all of a sudden they kicked me out and told me they had to get the baby out fast. I haven't heard anything since."

"Why didn't you call? I mean...sorry. You must have enough on your mind."

"Sadie..." Pip sniffled, speaking quietly now, "what if they both...die...and I'm left with...with nothing?"

"Oh my dear boy. God won't let that happen! I'll start a prayer chain immediately!"

But Pip knew it could happen. It happened to others, and God didn't save them. His entire childhood had been carved that way. As much as he believed in God and the power of prayer, doubts still surfaced. "I'd appreciate that. It helps to know that people care."

"People do care, Pip! I care!"

"Thank you!"

"Now, I want you to let me know the moment you hear something. Do you understand? If I don't hear back from you, I'll call."

"Okay." Pip told her, sniffling again, embarrassed for crying.

"How long has she been in surgery?"

"It's been over an hour."

"Okay, well try not to worry. I know that sounds cliché, but just spend the time praying, and I'll do the same. Now, I need to go start the prayer chain. Love you my boy."

"I love you too, Sadie." Pip ended the call and set his phone down beside him. He rubbed his temples with his palms, and paused for a moment. He knew Sadie was right and he needed to stay positive and pray as hard as he could. It's what he had been doing all along, but the doubts were creeping in fast with every moment that went by.

God in heaven, protect my wife and child, and let everything be okay!

Chapter 2

Sadie immediately called her friend Gladys who promised to continue the prayer chain by phone. She filled her in with all the details, said a prayer together with Gladys on the phone, and then hung up. Next she went on her computer and posted a status on Facebook for her Global Missions friends. Even though she wasn't too keen on social media the way the young people were, she knew it was the fastest and best method to get the word out.

It bothered her that Pip hadn't called, until she had. For a long time, she had been praying for him and Dinah. They seemed to be lost, displaced without family or friends, or even a church family. She realized not everyone thought church to be important, and yes, one could be a Christian without going, but it helped especially when you didn't have family.

It would break her heart if those two young people disconnected from her as well. She had to do something besides pray. Usually she stayed out of things and let God do the work, but sometimes it was time to act. She'd light a fire under the boards butt to hire a second maintenance man. Sadie picked up the phone and pressed in the numbers. "Hello, Brother Devin, Sadie here. Remember when I put in a request for a second maintenance man around here?"

"Sure sure." The elderly gentleman replied.

"Well, I was wondering. Has the board made a decision yet?"

The man on the other line hummed and hawed, and that same uncomfortable feeling Sadie got last time she called, crept in. She'd tried this before, and always got the run-a-round. What was going on, anyway?

"Well, Sadie," the old man spoke softly, all of a sudden, "since I have you on the phone, I might as well tell you. The board just met yesterday, and we were going to make it official. But..."

Sadie didn't like the sound of that. She felt her forehead start to perspire and her pulse thump like she was running a marathon. "But what, Brother Devin?"

"We...um, we're shutting you down?"

"What? Why?" Sadie couldn't believe what she was hearing. They couldn't just shut her down. The place belonged to Ben and Loretta not them. There never was a danger of the place closing down before. It was willed to Ben. Sure, after the fire, they had to go into debt to rebuild, but Ben and Loretta would have told her if the lodge was in trouble financially.

"I'm sorry Sadie," Brother Devin told her. "Ben wanted to tell you himself but he and Loretta left on a two-week European cruise this morning. He didn't want us to say anything until he had a chance to talk to you...and since you asked about hiring someone else, you put me in a hard spot. I shouldn't have said anything. You're upset aren't you?"

Sadie cleared her throat. "Of course I'm upset! I can't believe this."

"Please don't be upset."

How could she not be upset? The lodge was her job, and home. She couldn't have one without the other. What was she going to do now? "You're right, Devin, you shouldn't have said anything. Now what am I supposed to do to make a living? Where am I going to live?"

"Now Sadie..." The man fumbled his words. "I...um, oh dear. This is what Ben wanted to talk to you about. I'm sorry. I'll just say it. He wanted to make sure you understood that you don't have to move. It wasn't his decision to shut the Shining Star Ministries down, it was ours. We have decided to go in another direction, that's all. The actual physical building with still be functional. You needn't worry about that. You still have a home."

Just not a job.

"Okay, well I guess I'll wait until Ben calls me in a couple weeks to explain it all. I won't put you on the hot seat any longer Devin. If the board won't fund Shining Star Ministries anymore, then that is the way it is. I just need to find another job."

"And we will write you the best reference letter possible. Just say the word."

Sadie almost gasped. Did they realize where she was living? It was in the middle of nowhere in northern Canada. She may as well be on the moon, because jobs in the region were not exactly plentiful. And that wasn't the only concern she had, she was old, far too old to be sending out résumés and reference letters and hunting down work. It wasn't fair.

She should be retiring, not looking for another job. But retirement wasn't an option. It never was. She simply didn't make enough to save for a retirement fund. Working for a non-profit organization hadn't made her rich, it actually prevented her from having the necessities of life, sometimes.

But then she stopped herself. She was not going to be bitter. Shining Star Lodge had been a blessing for so many people, including herself. She wanted to remember it that way. But what was she going to do now? Living in a shell of a lodge without guests coming and going, would be a lonely life, not to mention a poor one. She either had to find a way to make a living, or be forced to move no matter how generous Ben and Loretta were with their place. They didn't have to let her live there. They could just up and sell, but it didn't sound like that's what they intended to do.

"Sadie?" The voice on the other end called out. "Are you still there?"

"Yes, I'm still here. I'm just thinking."

"Well, you needn't worry. You still have a place to live."

"Thank you, Devin, I appreciate you saying that, but I'm afraid it gives me little comfort. I'm still worried."

"Well don't be. Ben wouldn't want that. He'll call when he gets back. Anyway. I should run. I'll let you go, Sadie. Bye for now."

And with that, the phone went dead. Was that really the end of her job, the mission, everything? After all the lives they helped turn around, after all the work she had done with the young people that were sent to her, this was how it was going to end? Oh, how she wished she hadn't called. But then, she called to ask for a job for Pip. Now she couldn't offer him anything.

And the baby…oh, she better get praying about that baby. Her own problems would have to wait for now. There were more important things going on at the moment.

~~~~

Dinah came too, groggy and out of sorts. Her vision was blurry and she felt numb. Where was she? What was going on? Where was Pip? And... *the* baby? Panic rose in her chest and she tried to sit up, but none of her limbs responded. "Help!" she tried to scream, but only small squeaks came out.

"Oh, Mrs. Eaglefeather," a nearby voice spoke. "You're finally awake."

She heard some mumbling, then a group of nurses quickly gathered around her.

"You needn't try to get up. Your body is still numb from the anesthetic we gave you. You had a difficult time of it."

Dinah cleared her throat and tried to speak again. "Difficult?"

"Yes! It was touch and go there for a while, but you pulled through, somehow. You sure are a fighter. You put on quite the show for all those residents, but you wouldn't remember any of that, now would you. You were out cold."

She was right. She had no memory of that, only Pip sitting at her side in the labor and delivery ward. "Where's Pip?"

"Who?"

"My husband."

The nurse furrowed her brown, and that alerted Dinah immediately. She could tell something was on her mind.

"Mr. Eaglefeather went to the nursery. But he told me you weren't...married anymore. In fact, he said he hadn't seen you for nine months. Didn't even know you were pregnant."

"What? That's ridiculous?" Dinah replied, raising her raspy voice. "Why would he say that?" Apparently her panic had alerted the entire nursing staff to come running. They tried to calm her down but she wouldn't have any of it. She deserved to know what was going on. Why would Pip say they weren't married anymore?

"Dinah! Please, calm down!"

"NO! Not until you get my husband! I want to see my husband! I want to see my baby. BRING ME MY BABY!"

Suddenly sirens went off in the hospital hallway, and immediately most of the nurses left. Dinah could hear the 'code pink' announcement broadcasted all over the ward. Tears formed in her eyes. "What does that mean? What is code pink?"

"Um...nothing dear! Don't you worry your pretty little head," the older nurse tried to calm her by closing the double doors to the hallway, blocking the noise.

"Then, tell me what's wrong?"

"Nothing's wrong! Just ignore the noise. All you have to be concerned with is your baby. You have a beautiful healthy girl. A real sweetheart. She doesn't have your coloring, but she's got gorgeous dark skin like your ex husb—"

"I told you he's not my ex, he's my husband!"

The nurse frowned. "Well, whatever you call him. He followed the baby to the nursery, but we checked his I.D first, so don't worry. He was, in fact, Mr. Eaglefeather. Tall thin fella with a silver smile?"

"Silver smile? What are you talking about?" Dinah couldn't believe this. Did they give her baby to the wrong dad?

"You know, his silver front tooth?"

"What? NO! That's not him. He's never been to the dentist in his life."

The nurse chuckled like she didn't believe her. "I'm sure we'll get this all sorted out eventually. I just started my shift, so what do I know? You've been out of it for a while, so you're probably a little fuzzy."

"Fuzzy? I think I know my own husband!"

"I'm sure you do," the nurse said, shushing her as she took Dinah's vitals, and looked at her watch. "You need to calm down, my dear. Your baby needs a healthy mama."

Tears rolled down Dinah's cheek as she flopped her head on the pillow, frustrated and worried that they gave her baby to the wrong dad. A baby. I have a baby girl. Where was her baby? Where was Pip? All these unanswered questions made Dinah's head hurt. And she could barely keep her eyelids open. They had given her something and now she was drifting off to sleep again. No! She didn't want to, but it was too hard to fight. Maybe when she wakes, this will all be a bad dream?

~~~~

"My staff already told you officer." Dr. Uric lowered his voice. "The guy had I.D and everything. He was definitely the father. I don't know why he would have taken the newborn out of the hospital without consent, but it's not an abduction. Maybe he didn't understand that we keep newborns for at least twenty-four hours?"

The balding officer was busy taking notes and finally looked up. "So you're telling me there was no need to call us at all?"

"Well, yes and no. I mean, it's protocol when a newborn goes missing, but she's with the father for sure. Our security cameras prove that. He took her out the front doors shortly after she was brought to the nursery to get weighed and measured. But there was a shift change, and I'll have to call the night staff back in for questioning if you insist this is an abduction. They aren't going to be very happy with me."

The officer shook his head. "Fine then. We'll check the security cameras for now, but let us know when the mother is awake. We'd like to speak with her about the father."

"I'm sure that will clear everything up. The natives around here are different with their cultural beliefs." Dr Uric tried to smile. "He probably wanted to hold her up to the moon or something. Who knows. I'm sure he'll be back. The mother is in I.C.U for Pete's sake. He wouldn't just leave her."

TO CONTINUE READING DEEP BAY LEGACY, PLEASE GO TO AMAZON.COM TO PURCHASH IT.

ABOUT THE AUTHOR

Award-winning author Kathleen Morris writes Christian fiction, mystery, suspense, and thrillers, to spread biblical truths around the world through her many flawed characters she creates. Her hope is to show that we all deserve God's unconditional love. Kathleen's debut novel titled, *Deep Bay Vengeance* is her first in the *Deep Bay Series,* with *Deep Bay Relic*, and *Deep Bay Legacy,* to conclude the trilogy. Her next novel is *The Prion Attachment,* first in the *Blood War Series,* followed by book two titled, *Blood Purge.* When she's not writing, she enjoys spending time with her husband Barry and their three grown children at her home in Saskatchewan, Canada. For more on Kathleen Morris please check out her Amazon Author page.

BOOKS BY KATHLEEN MORRIS

Try the new *Blood War* series.
The Prion Attatchement
Blood Purge

####